"Not hungry?" Bubba asked softly

'Just nervous."

"Try to eat a little more. It's only seven-thirty.
I promise not to start anything before nine."

The smile Melanie tried to give him was so weak
that her lips trembled. "I'm sorry, Bubba. I'm the
one who came to you, and I just don't know if
I can go through with it."

He set his glass down, the pizza obviously forgotten.
"Mel, what will make this easy for you?"

"Remember when I said maybe we could just go
upstairs and..."

"In the dark," he said.

She laughed, and it sounded more like a whimper.
"Bubba," she whispered. "I wish I were more
sophisticated. I wish everything weren't such a big
deal, that I could just do things and not think them
to death."

Taking her hand, he began to stroke her wrist. "Why
don't we just go on upstairs and see how it goes?"

ABOUT THE AUTHOR

Elda Minger became a writer via a circuitous
route. Through the years she has worked in
several bookstores, cleaned houses in Beverly
Hills, ushered in theaters, sung for her supper
on Hollywood Boulevard and even appeared in
two movies. Born in and now residing again in
Hollywood, California, Elda has lived in many
parts of the United States, as well as in such
foreign countries as Italy.

Books by Elda Minger

HARLEQUIN AMERICAN ROMANCE
12—UNTAMED HEART
95—ANOTHER CHANCE AT HEAVEN
106—TOUCHED BY LOVE
117—SEIZE THE FIRE
133—BACHELOR MOTHER

These books may be available at your local bookseller.

Don't miss any of our special offers. Write to us at the
following address for information on our newest releases.

Harlequin Reader Service
P.O. Box 52040, Phoenix, AZ 85072-2040
Canadian address: P.O. Box 2800, Postal Station A,
5170 Yonge St., Willowdale, Ont. M2N 6J3

Bachelor Mother

ELDA MINGER

Harlequin Books

TORONTO • NEW YORK • LONDON
AMSTERDAM • PARIS • SYDNEY • HAMBURG
STOCKHOLM • ATHENS • TOKYO • MILAN

To Billy Katz,
for five of my happiest years.
May there be many more. I love you.

Published January 1986

First printing November 1985

ISBN 0-373-16133-6

Chapter One

Do it.

Melanie Randell twirled the delicate wineglass in her hands. She'd thought some Chablis would give her Dutch courage, but she'd been wrong.

Bubba won't laugh at you. Just explain the situation to him.

But this was so personal.

She sighed and set her glass down. How had she managed to get herself into this mess? It was a simple quirk of fate, a trick played by Mother Nature. Here she'd thought she had all the time in the world, only to have the proverbial rug pulled right out from underneath her feet.

So ask him, dodo. The worst thing he can do is tell you to forget it.

Melanie got up off the couch in her living room, then walked over to the sliding glass door leading to her patio and redwood deck. Sliding the glass open, she walked to the edge of the deck and leaned on the railing. Glancing over at Bubba's house next door, she smiled.

Soft rock music escaped from an open window. There were lights on low in Bubba's living room, and as Melanie listened, she heard soft, throaty feminine laughter.

She could picture Bubba with his latest conquest. She'd be the type who filled out a brief bikini to perfection. Just as Bubba epitomized the all-American surfer, the women he went out with looked like beach bunnies—Annette Funnicello at her best. She'd always teased him about the succession of Gidgets in his life, and he took her ribbing with good-natured tolerance. Nothing ruffled Bubba.

What you're going to ask him to do just might.

Another breathy giggle floated across the cool evening air. June in Southern California could be uncomfortably warm, but as both their houses were less than six blocks from the beach in Santa Monica, she and Bubba always escaped the worst of the heat.

Melanie stared up at the sky and tried to will herself into action.

What if he says no? You've already exhausted all your other options.

As quickly as the first thought entered her mind, the second followed.

But he's always been there for you. So why wouldn't he help you now?

It was true. Her older brother Donnie had dragged Bubba—Robert Jonathan Williams, actually, but they'd always called him Bubba—home with him one day after school, and it seemed as if he'd never left. They'd both been in the third grade, and sat next to each other in the classroom. Melanie, six years younger than her brother, had never known a time when Bubba wasn't around. She'd toddled after him as a baby, annoyed him as a little girl, and gone to him with boy problems as an adolescent. He'd rumpled her hair or swatted her butt playfully. He'd even taken her side against Donnie a few times, especially when she'd insisted she was old enough to leave home and start living her own life.

She glanced quickly at her watch, squinting against the soft light from the living room. Ten forty-six. It looked as if Gidget was going to spend the night.

You can't just barge in and interrupt them.

Melanie sighed.

That's right; look for the perfect time. Only there never is a perfect time. Ask him now.

As if someone else was responsible for her movements, Melanie walked back into her house and locked the sliding door. Grabbing a light blue hand-knit sweater, she pulled it over her head and reached for her keys.

Hesitating for just a moment, she glanced quickly into the mirror in the hallway.

You look fine. Her long blond hair was mussed and she hadn't bothered with makeup. There were slight shadows underneath her deep blue eyes, evidence of several sleepless nights. As she studied herself, she bit her lip, still not sure that what she was about to do was the smartest thing.

Without giving herself time to think too much, she walked quickly to the front door and let herself out.

The walk to Bubba's front door took less than a minute. Melanie rubbed her damp palms against her faded jeans and rang the bell.

The first ring didn't bring Bubba to the door. She waited almost thirty seconds, then knocked.

Listening carefully, she heard footsteps. As Bubba swung the door open, she stepped back.

"Hey, Mel! I haven't seen you for at least a couple of hours."

He smiled, and she felt her muscles relax. He wasn't mad at her for interrupting him during a private moment. It *was* Friday night, after all.

Bubba leaned against the doorjamb, his entire manner relaxed. He was wearing a faded pair of cut-offs, but his chest and feet were bare. His muscled chest was covered with dark blond hair, and Melanie noticed he needed a haircut. Perhaps she could do it for him on Sunday.

When he spoke again, she realized she hadn't said anything.

"Mel?" He touched her upper arm gently. "You look like hell."

She couldn't say what she had to say in public, on his front steps. Something this momentous—well, at least they should be sitting down.

She took a deep breath. "Bubba, could I talk to you for a moment?"

He looked puzzled. "Sure. Listen, Mel, if it's about Henry getting in your garbage, I—"

"No, this has nothing to do with your cat. But it's—" She glanced beyond Bubba, down the hall to the softly lit living room. "It's kind of private."

"Okay, I get it. Come on inside." He stepped back, allowing her to walk in front of him down the short hall to the living room. Melanie recognized Joanie, one of Bubba's girlfriends, curled up on the couch. The remains of a pizza in a cardboard container and two empty wineglasses were scattered over the top of the coffee table.

"Hi, Mel." She didn't look up from the glossy magazine she was reading.

"Hi, Joanie. I like your hair."

None of Bubba's girlfriends looked at her as a threat, probably because she and Bubba were in and out of each other's houses on a regular basis. "Living out of each other's pockets," as her brother Don had put it once.

Bubba disappeared into the kitchen and came back with another glass of wine. He handed it to Melanie, then picked up Joanie's glass.

"Nope. I'm leaving." Joanie swung her long, tanned legs off the couch and stood up gracefully. She flashed a dazzling smile at Bubba.

"Walk me to the door, honey. A day at the beach with you has just about fried my brains."

"Joanie, you're going to give me a swelled head," Bubba teased.

"Among other things, I hope."

Mel laughed, then sat down on the couch as Joanie picked up her oversize bag and sweatshirt. Once they were in the hallway, Melanie closed her eyes and set her glass down on the coffee table. She tried not to eavesdrop, but she heard Bubba give Joanie a good-bye kiss. She knew he would stand in the open doorway and make sure she got safely into her car and started it up.

When the door closed, Mel jumped.

Bubba walked into the living room with the grace of a natural athlete. She watched him as he turned off the stereo and came back to the couch. He sat down next to her, his arm along the top of the couch as he caught a strand of her hair.

"So what's bugging you, Mel?"

She opened her mouth to speak but nothing came out.

He studied her face, and she could tell he was worried. "Mel, is it Phillip?"

She was sure her face reflected her disgust as she reached for her wine. "No. That's been over for almost a week."

"I thought he hadn't been coming over as much."

"Ah, he's ancient history," she replied, taking a sip of her wine. She had to do something to stifle her nervousness.

"Is something wrong at work?" he asked.

"No, everything's fine." This was getting nowhere. The way she was orchestrating this conversation, she and Bubba would be playing twenty questions all night.

Get to the point.

"Actually, I wanted to ask you a really big personal favor."

"Anything." He squeezed her shoulder.

"Bubba, don't agree until you hear what it is."

"Aw, come on, babe, you know I'd do anything for you. Is it another problem with Don?"

She smiled, touched by his loyalty. How many times had Bubba gotten her out of a mess while they were growing up? It was ironic that their very personal pattern was once again being repeated.

She set her wineglass down and looked him straight in the eye. "It's serious, Bubba. And it's something very important to me."

"Okay." He was silent, waiting for her to continue.

She looked away, unable to meet his eyes. "Six months ago, I went to my doctor for a checkup. He told me I only have a year to—"

"Oh, my God." Before she could continue, she was enfolded in a pair of warm, hard arms. His chin was on top of her head as he raised one hand and stroked her hair. "God, Mel."

She broke away from him, but he didn't release her completely from the circle of his arms. "No, it's nothing like that."

Bubba looked truly shaken. His deeply tanned face was pale, his blue-gray eyes dark with emotion. "Then what is it? You only have a year to—"

"Get pregnant." She finished the sentence for him, relieved it was finally out in the open.

"What?" Bubba looked thunderstruck.

She took advantage of his silence to quickly fill him in on the details.

"My gynecologist found an ovarian tumor. It's nothing fatal, but he told me that if I had any intentions of having a family, it was best if I got pregnant within the year."

There was a short silence, then Bubba said softly, "And if you don't?"

Her shoulders slumped as she looked down at her hands in her lap. It hurt, putting her worst fears into words. "Then I take the chance I may never be able to have children."

"Oh, no, Mel."

She knew Bubba was aware of how it hurt her. When she was a child, hadn't she always been surrounded by her dolls and stuffed animals? Nurturing, her friends called her. She'd never doubted that someday she wanted to become a mother, have children. But at twenty-six, she'd thought she had plenty of time.

"You're sure about this?" he asked.

She nodded her head. "I got a second opinion, and a third." She ran her fingers through her hair, the gesture tired. "I was so scared, then so angry. I kept thinking, why did it have to happen to me?"

He gave her a brief, hard hug, then released her. "So that's why Phillip hit the road, right? He didn't want an instant family."

"Yeah. He told me—he said he'd thought about maybe one child, to keep me happy, but not until his practice was better established."

"What a first-class ass." Bubba reached for his wineglass and took a sip. "So you want me to go talk to this jerk, huh?"

It took her a second to understand his meaning, and when she did, she grimaced. Why was he sometimes so dense? Why hadn't he offered, made this easier for her?

Summoning up all her courage, she blurted out her thoughts.

"Bubba, I want you to get me pregnant."

"Get you *what*?" Wine spewed out of his mouth, all over the front of his cutoffs.

Had it been another time, Melanie would have laughed. Now she seemed close to tears.

When she started to speak, her sentences were rapid, as if she were afraid he'd cut her off, send her home.

"Bubba, I've tried *everything*! When I first found out, I'd only been dating Phillip for three months. I thought he was the one that, with time, would love me enough to marry me, and then we could start a family. I gave us six more months, then I had to say something. But when I told him, he just left."

Bubba started to say something, but her eyes beseeched him to let her continue.

"I went to a singles' bar last night with Alicia. She thought I should just take someone home and well, never let him know." Her expression was anguished. Bubba reached out, clasping both her hands between his.

"I couldn't do it. Not with a stranger. It just didn't seem right, and what would I tell little What's-Her-Name when she asked me? That I met her father one night at a bar, but he never stuck around?"

She was fighting back tears, and he hurt with her. Funny how all the women he knew didn't want children but could have them so easily. And Mel—

"You're sure you want a child?" he asked.

Her eyes were brimming as she looked at him, and he handed her a paper napkin off the coffee table.

"I've never been more sure of anything! Everything else in life has been a big decision, but I've always known I wanted children."

Something in her tone of voice tore at his emotions. He knew she was telling him the truth. As a little girl, Mel had been fascinated with babies. The youngest child in a large family, she'd had plenty of practice with cousins and, recently, with both her sisters' children.

She'd make someone a terrific mother.

"Do we go to a doctor or something?" Now he was awkward, not knowing what to do. He wasn't even sure he could do it. How exactly did a guy approach this sort of problem?

"Well..." Now Mel seemed awkward. "I read up on everything: artificial insemination, adoption. Bubba, there's so much red tape, I thought it would be easier if we just took things into our own hands."

He tried to laugh at her choice of words, but he found his breath was lodged in his throat. "Mel, I feel kind of strange about this."

"Couldn't you just pretend I was Joanie?"

"No. I don't think I have that good an imagination." The minute he saw the expression on her face, he regretted his choice of words. "Hey, Mel, I didn't mean it that way. I mean, Joanie is just someone I have fun with. She knows it and she feels the same way. But with you..." His words trailed off. He wasn't really sure what he'd been about to say. When Melanie touched his shoulder, he looked up.

"You don't have to do anything besides getting me pregnant. We can go to a lawyer, make everything legal. I wouldn't ask you for child support or try to trick you into marrying me."

"Hey, cut it out! I know you, Mel. You wouldn't pull any stunt like that! And we don't need to go to any lawyer."

"No, I'd feel better if we did. I want everything to be up front. I don't want to cause you any more trouble than I have to."

"What will you tell your family?" He could just picture Donnie's reaction.

"The truth. *After* I've started to show. Then I'll be too far along for any alternate suggestions."

"You're really serious."

"Yeah. There's just no other way."

"When did you...ah, if we do this, when did you want to..." He couldn't seem to make himself say the words.

He noticed she was very careful not to look at him as she replied.

"I've been taking my temperature every morning. Saturday night would be perfect."

"*This* Saturday?" *Tomorrow?* He felt as if he were choking.

Mel stood up and began to pace restlessly around the living room. He could sense her nervousness and knew she was deeply upset. He was about to get up off the couch when she whirled on him.

"I can't believe I asked you!" Her color was high, and he knew she was embarrassed. "It's a stupid idea, Bubba. I want you to forget this entire conversation ever happened."

"Come on, Mel, that's no way to approach our problem."

"*My* problem, not yours. I'm sorry, Bubba. I shouldn't have gotten you mixed up in this mess. You're a nice guy. I know you're feeling sorry for me."

"Hey, Mel, come on! This isn't like you."

"This whole *evening* isn't like me." She stopped pacing abruptly and met his eyes. "I've got to go. Ridiculous. This has got to be the most ridiculous idea I've ever had in my life. So stupid." She was muttering to herself as she stomped off down his short hall and threw open the front door.

"Mel!" He got up and ran quickly to the door.

She was walking briskly across the short expanse of lawn that separated the two houses.

"Mel, I'll come over in the morning and we'll talk, okay?" he called out.

"I want you to forget this entire evening ever happened!"

He watched as she slammed her screen door. Then silence descended.

He sighed. *Forget this evening? That's as impossible as riding a thirty-foot wave with a boogie board.*

MOONLIGHT FILTERED through the curtains in Melanie's bedroom, making patterns across the patchwork quilt.

She glanced at the luminous dial of the clock. *Almost four in the morning and I still can't sleep.*

Melanie turned over on her side and bunched the pillow underneath her head. Alicia had called and left a message on her answering machine, imploring her to tell her what Bubba had decided. She hadn't called her friend back. It seemed too personal, somehow, to tell Alicia what had happened tonight.

I wonder how most couples decide to have a child, she thought sleepily. How wonderful if she'd simply had a loving husband who'd say, "Of course we'll have a child. I want to have children just as much as you do."

She was surprised at the tear that slipped slowly down her cheek. As confident as she'd sounded with Bubba, inside she was terrified. Who was she to bring a child into the world, a child with only a mother? Didn't every child deserve a father?

Sometimes there aren't any choices.

She thought of the smallest bedroom in her house, just down the hall from the master bedroom. Over the past six months, she'd slowly transformed it. Whenever she'd been depressed over the problem facing her, she'd worked on the little room. It was painted a sunny yellow. She'd put up white ruffled curtains in both windows. Large white shelves, big enough for plenty of toys, ran along two of the walls. There was a dresser she'd refinished and painted white, a mobile she'd bought on impulse that had tiny teddy bears sitting on stuffed stars and clouds. She'd even bought a grow chart with an ostrich on it.

She'd crocheted two baby afghans and bought a small crib-size patchwork quilt. She'd even placed her own beloved teddy bear, all moth-eaten but carefully stitched up, in a place of honor in the middle of the top shelf.

There's so very much I want to give you, she thought quietly, thinking of the child she wanted. *So much I want to share.*

But as badly as she wanted a child, was she doing the right thing to Bubba? Was she asking too much in the name of friendship?

You were wrong to even ask him.

She knew he lived a casual, easygoing life. Bubba's house was always open to all his friends. His large weekend parties were famous. During the summer months, he had a group of friends who made up two opposing volleyball teams, and they played twice a week in his large backyard.

Everyone knew Bubba. Even the senior citizens on the block speculated on "when that nice young man was going to settle down."

Melanie knew it wasn't going to happen for a long time. Bubba liked his life-style; he made that very clear to the legions of women who dated him. He liked to pick up and go, make trips up the coast at a moment's notice. He still surfed, even though he was thirty-two, and his last vacation had been to Hawaii to catch the big wave.

He'd kept almost all his friends from his childhood, including her brother Don. He was a congenial host, an easygoing date, a sensitive friend.

It was clear to anyone with eyes that he was a totally free spirit.

She turned over one last time, thoroughly exhausted. Melanie fell asleep, and she dreamed of Bubba on the beach with a flock of children, teaching them all to surf.

YOU ARE GETTING DRUNK.

Bubba swirled the last of the wine in his glass, then tipped it up and let it splash down into his mouth. After Mel had left, he'd gone back to the couch and tried to watch a late-night talk show.

It had been impossible. He hadn't been able to get Mel out of his mind.

Are you crazy? What do you think you are, some kind of machine? A superstud baby maker?

He set his glass down on the coffee table, rolled over onto his stomach and groaned.

How would you ever go to bed with her? You've known her since she was in diapers.

Saturday night. Tomorrow. Tomorrow night Mel had wanted him to throw off his clothes and jump her bones just as if she were a casual date. His dates were women who wanted physical sensation, pleasure and release. Someone who definitely knew the score, who wouldn't be hurt.

Would I hurt her by doing this? The thought had plagued him for hours. Yet he couldn't bear the thought of her picking up a stranger in a bar.

If there was a woman in his life he knew inside and out, it was Melanie Randell. He'd practically lived at her house and watched her grow up. He knew how much she loved children and animals, how she hated Japanese food. He was also well aware of the stubborn streak of independence that surfaced in her fights with her overprotective big brother. Don could be a pain at times.

But more important, he knew that underneath that strong-as-steel exterior was a sensitive woman who felt deeply. It had cost her a lot to come to him with her problem. He'd seen it in her face, how she'd hated asking him if he'd father a child for her. She'd been as awkward, as embarrassed, as he had been.

So do you do it or not?

He closed his eyes as a subtle wave of dizziness washed over him.

*Great planning. You should be getting a good night's sleep, popping zinc pills and pumping iron, not getting dead drunk and lying on the couch at—*he raised his head and blearily eyed the clock on the wall—*four in the morning.*

He rested his cheek against a cushion and stared at the far wall, the colors in the curtains blurring. There was no way he was going to let Mel make love to a perfect stranger. What if she ended up with a real loony tune, someone who messed her up? Or what if the guy found out and tried to take the child away from her?

I don't think I can do it.

He cursed Phillip fluently as he slowly rose to his feet and began to climb the steps to his bedroom.

It was a mess. Though he hired a cleaning lady to come in once a week, and was quite adept as far as cooking and doing dishes went, he tended to let his bedroom mushroom out of control like a nuclear blast. There were dirty clothes piled in one corner, last weeks' Sunday paper in another. The bed was un-made.

It didn't look inviting.

Well, you aren't going to be getting any sleep. You might as well clean it up.

Bubba stalked into the bathroom and filled the sink with cold water. Gritting his teeth, he stuck his head in the sink for as long as he could stand it. When he finally surfaced and reached for a towel, his head felt slightly clearer. This accomplished, he began to straighten his bedroom.

One look at this and she'd run out screaming. No mother would want her child to inherit messy genes. He sighed. *Just tell her you don't think you can do it.*

Chapter Two

When Melanie opened her eyes the next morning, she wondered why she felt so disoriented, so out of sorts. Then she remembered. Bubba. Last night.

Why did you ever ask him?

It was a strange request, even of a best friend. With all her heart, Melanie wished she could have done everything in a more emotionally logical order: fallen in love, courted, married, had a child.

But in her circumstance, there simply wasn't time.

She lay back among the crisp, white sheets and remembered her entire evening at Bubba's house. Obviously, she'd caught him off guard. He'd thought she wanted him to tell Phil to shape up. She found herself smiling at the thought of Bubba marching into Phil's law office and demanding he marry her. She doubted anything would change Phil's mind. The expression on his face when she explained her predicament had been so clearly obvious. He'd waited just a second too long before he responded, then had been so careful to choose the right words. But Phil's hesitation had answered her question long before he began to speak.

And anyway, what could she expect from a man she'd been dating only nine months? It wasn't as if there ever had been a promise on either side. He'd seen her at a party, asked her out. Enjoyed her company. Found her attractive.

There had never been a discussion about commitment, until Melanie had reached the end of her six-month self-imposed time limit. Even then, she'd been reluctant to present her problem to Phil.

You always knew he wasn't going to commit himself to you. Perhaps you even went out with him for that reason. He'd been safe. The perfect gentleman. So careful.

She swung out of bed. *I don't want someone who's careful. I want someone who's reckless enough to lay his heart on the line.*

Glancing at the clock, she was surprised to find it was almost noon. She rarely slept that late, being a morning person.

Apologize to Bubba. Ask him to dinner.

She needed to distract herself from the anxiety that was steadily building inside her. So she began methodically to strip the bed.

There was nothing like housework to bring a person back to earth.

Three hours later, Melanie stood back and surveyed her bedroom. Her housecleaning had been rapid, just the quickest once-over. There was a chicken cooking slowly in a Crockpot in her kitchen.

The least she could do was feed Bubba dinner.

She felt as if her entire body were exposed, a bundle of nerves and pure raw embarrassment. Her skin seemed glaringly sensitive; her head ached.

Melanie closed her eyes and pressed her fingers against her temples. As if in answer to her unspoken question, the phone rang.

She picked up the receiver with shaky fingers. "Hello?" For an instant she hoped it was Bubba. Then she could tell him she'd been temporarily insane last night and hadn't meant a word she'd said.

It was Alicia.

"Well? What happened? What did he say?'

Melanie could picture her friend and business partner on the other end of the line. Alicia would have her legs propped carelessly on her breakfast-room table. Her dark, straight hair was cut to her shoulders, and her brown eyes were endlessly inquisitive. At first, Alicia's blunt, personal questions had set her teeth on edge. Then, when they knew each other better and Melanie had figured out her friend wasn't offended if she chose not to answer, Melanie had relaxed.

"Not everyone has the guts to ask the questions I do," Alicia had once told her. "And most of the time I get answers."

But sometimes, particularly on a day like today, her friend's habit of intense scrutiny could be wearing.

"He didn't say anything. I didn't ask him." Melanie crossed her fingers in her lap, hating having to lie. But she just wasn't up to discussing with Alicia the evening ahead.

"Melanie! You had almost all night to ask him. Are you sure you want to go through with it?"

"No, I'm not." That part was truthful at least.

Alicia considered this for just a second. She was like a small terrier worrying a bone. After a short silence, she asked, "Do you want to go out with me tonight, hit a few bars?"

"No. I'm going to get some work done."

"Ah! You can't use that excuse with me! We have more than enough sweaters in stock." Alicia had been the one to talk her into going into business for herself. Together they ran a small boutique on Pier Avenue that specialized in hand-knit sweaters.

Melanie clenched the phone tightly, dismayed to find her hand was starting to sweat. "Ali, I really think I just need some time alone to think things through."

Her friend's voice was suddenly gentle. "You know you don't have that much more time." When Melanie didn't answer, she said, "Well, I guess one more night won't hurt. I'll be back tonight around midnight if you want to give me a call." Alicia hesitated a moment, then said, "You know, last night I ran into a woman Bubba used to go out with, at a party my dating service gave."

"Oh?" Melanie forced her tone to remain calm. She wanted nothing more than to rip apart her freshly made bed and climb underneath the covers. But a person could only ignore the world for so long.

"Yeah. I asked her what he was like in bed."

"Alicia!"

Her friend was utterly unperturbed. "She got this disgustingly dreamy look on her face and said he was the best, the most *passionate* lover she'd ever had. She said he really knew how to please a woman and that when he—"

"Ali, I don't want to hear any more. I've decided—" She thought quickly. "I've decided I don't want to spoil the special friendship I have with Bubba, so I think I'm going to do it your way."

"Love with the proper stranger? I *love* it!"

"Yeah, that's it. So I'll call you tomorrow and we'll talk about places I can go to meet men."

"I still think you should join my video dating service."

"We'll talk about it tomorrow, okay?"

When Melanie hung up the phone, she covered her face with her hands. Whatever had possessed her to ask Bubba to play surrogate father? Now, more than ever, she was convinced she'd done the wrong thing.

Not one to sink into despair if there was something she could do about it, she picked up the phone and dialed Bubba's number.

IT SOUNDED as if someone were tap dancing on his head.

Bubba groaned as the phone shrilled again, and he wondered why he hadn't thought to disconnect it before he fell asleep. Who could be calling him at this ungodly hour?

"Hullo?" he mumbled into the receiver.

"Bubba? It's me."

"Mel!" He sat up in bed, blinking against the slight light his curtains let in. "Are you okay?" He was about to ask her what was wrong when she rushed ahead.

"Bubba, I—I'm sorry I asked you last night. I was—I was really depressed when I came over, and I guess I was just crazy. It's a stupid idea. I don't want to wreck our friendship, and I'd like you to come over for dinner tonight. *Just* for dinner."

He was wide awake now, even if his brain seemed slightly fuzzy. "But I thought you said you had to get pregnant." She wasn't making sense.

"I know I said that, but I shouldn't have asked you. Now look, I'll solve my problem some other way, but in the meantime, do you want to come over tonight?"

"And have you sleep with some stranger? I can't let that happen!"

He could hear her sigh over the phone. "Bubba, we're not having the same conversation. I *promise* you I won't go to some sleazy bar and pick up Mr. Goodbar. But I really think I was way out of line to ask you."

"I don't. What are friends for?"

"Bubba!"

He rubbed his forehead wearily. "Mel, I know you're scared about this whole thing. You have enough to worry about without having to look for a decent guy. I don't want you sleeping with some creep just so you can have a baby!"

"But I can't sleep with you!" she said desperately.

"Look, we've got to be reasonable about this. If you sleep with some stranger, how do you know how your kid is going to turn out?" Bubba thought furiously; then he remembered an article he'd read in his dentist's office last week. "Besides, what if your baby gets sick and you have to know something about his heredity? I'll always be around to answer your questions, and if I don't know, I can call up my mother.''

He knew he was beginning to make sense to her when she didn't answer him right away. Knowing he had to convince her before she changed her mind, he spoke carefully, softly.

"Mel, if it's any consolation to you, I'm just as scared as you are. I'm worried about whether I'm doing the right thing. I don't want to hurt you. But as far as I can see, you have a couple of choices, and the best one is to let me help you.''

"You really think so?" She sounded as if she were close to tears.

"I know so.'' He forced his voice to sound more assured than he felt. "Now forget about fixing me dinner. I'm taking you out. And don't worry, I'm going to take care of everything.''

"Bubba, I really love you.''

"I love you, too, Mel. And I know how much this means to you.''

"Thank you,'' she whispered. Then she hung up.

He lay in bed, satisfied with the way he'd convinced her until he remembered that right before he'd fallen asleep early that morning he'd been determined to tell her he couldn't go through with it.

Turning his head slightly, he stared into a pair of golden feline eyes. Henry, an enormous white cat that he'd rescued from his garbage can almost a year ago, licked his nose and then bit it gently.

Bubba tapped the cat's nose lightly to make him let go. "Why the hell didn't you wake me up this morning, huh? Then I would have had a clear brain by the time Mel called.''

As he started to get out of bed, Henry butted his head against his chest and meowed pitifully.

"I know, breakfast." He glanced at the clock on his bedside table. "Make that lunch."

As Bubba stood up, Henry hit the floor with a loud thwack and followed him down the stairs and into the kitchen.

WHEN THE DOORBELL RANG, Melanie tensed.

Seven o'clock. Bubba was certainly punctual. She studied herself quickly in the hallway mirror. The peach-and-white cotton sundress set off her tan. It had an elasticized, strapless top and a wide sash nipped in the waist.

Her hair was loose, and it waved slightly as it fell below her shoulders. She'd made up her face carefully to hide the ravages of a practically sleepless night, and the sandals she had on were comfortable.

Here goes.

She opened the door, a nervous smile on her face. Bubba was standing on her front steps, dressed in a pair of jeans and a light blue button-down shirt. He had a bouquet of yellow roses in his hand.

"Oh, Bubba, how pretty! Just let me get a vase." She turned away quickly, touched by his thoughtfulness. He followed her into the kitchen and helped her get a vase out of one of her kitchen cupboards.

"They're from Gabe across the street," he informed her, referring to one of the old ladies who lived on the block. "She called me up and told me Henry was digging around in her flower bed. When I came over to get him and told her I was coming to dinner tonight, she insisted I take some of her roses.''

Melanie laughed, surprised at how the tension seemed to be leaving her body. She could just picture Gabe chasing Henry with her broom. Bubba's cat was a well-known mischief maker in the neighborhood.

''I'll be sure to thank her for her thoughtfulness.'' She placed the vase on her coffee table, then turned around and looked up at him. ''Look, Bubba, I have to tell you something before I lose my nerve.''

He was studying her carefully.

Melanie moistened her lips with the tip of her tongue, suddenly nervous. ''Let's just have dinner tonight, okay?''

''Mel, I don't want you to have to—''

She laid a hand on his chest. ''I *promise* you I won't go after any strangers in bars without letting you know first. Deal?''

She could see him visibly relaxing. ''Deal.''

''I hope you like my version of sweet-and-sour chicken.''

''I thought we were going out.''

''Uh-uh. You deserve a good, home-cooked meal after what I put you through last night.''

Bubba sighed. ''Anything you cook will be fine with me.''

He looked out of place in her kitchen. She'd decorated it in a country motif, and Bubba just didn't seem to mix in with the white ruffled curtains and the embroidered sampler hanging on one of the walls. He was so big, so athletic. He looked like the kind of man who needed room to move around. Her little kitchen didn't afford that much space.

"There's a bottle of wine in the refrigerator," she said. "Everything should be ready; so we can eat in about fifteen minutes."

Bubba's head was already in her refrigerator. "Mel, you've got enough here to feed any army!"

She laughed. "It's just that I hate to go to the market more than once a year." Sometimes she was secretly ashamed of her strong streak of domesticity. While most of her friends confessed they hated to stay home in the evenings and cook, Melanie loved her little house. Actually, it belonged to her brother Don, and he had been delighted to rent it to her as a tax shelter. She enjoyed having people over for small dinner parties. She liked to nurture those she loved.

Bubba reached inside for the wine and shut the refrigerator door carefully. As he searched one of her kitchen drawers for a corkscrew, he said, "Well, at least you eat properly. You'll have to be on a special diet when you're—" He stopped, as if he were suddenly embarrassed, and concentrated on opening the wine.

They drank in silence, then Melanie quickly dished up the Oriental chicken over rice. They sat at her kitchen table and Bubba ate thoughtfully, but he didn't quite meet her eyes.

We've never been this uncomfortable before, she thought miserably. *If only you hadn't opened your big mouth last night.*

After she cleared away the dishes, Melanie got out the chocolate mousse she'd spent the afternoon making. Bubba's favorite. It was a peace offering.

"This is really great, Mel."

She smiled, relaxing at last. He seemed more like the Bubba she was used to.

Sitting back in her chair and studying Bubba as he looked out her kitchen window, Melanie could understand why so many women had gone out with him, given their hearts to him, and still remained friends afterward. There was something special about Bubba—he was emotionally so open, so thoughtful of other people.

His looks certainly didn't hinder him. She liked the way his hair was bleached by the sun, the way the wind and saltwater and strong outdoor light had carved expressive lines into his face. He was a handsome man; his dark blue-gray eyes were alive with feeling.

As if sensing that she was staring at him, he looked at her.

"What are you thinking about?"

It would have never occurred to her to hide her thoughts from Bubba.

"I was wondering why you never got married," she admitted. "Have you ever been in love?"

"No." He sat back in his chair, regarding her with a serious expression. She noticed the slight tightening around his mouth. "It wasn't exactly a secret that my parents were one of the great mismatches of all time. I can't remember either of them ever being in the same room without fighting." He picked up his dessert spoon, studied it, then set it back down. "I always wondered why your parents were so kind, letting me hang out at your house. I practically lived there my last two years in high school."

"You were fun to have around," she said, teasing him, hating to see his hurt. Bubba had rarely talked about his parents, but she and her sisters and brothers had known. No one had been surprised when they divorced after Bubba left for college.

"I loved being with all of you." He smiled, and it seemed to Melanie he was making a conscious effort to change the subject, away from the depressing topic. "Anyway, I have a bet going with your brother Don."

"With Donnie?" She laughed. "This has to be good."

His eyes were laughing as he said, "We have a bet. The first guy to bite the dust pays up—five hundred dollars."

Melanie felt her mouth fall open. "Are you serious?"

"Absolutely."

"When did you decide this?"

"Senior year. Right after Don broke up with Liz."

"Ah, yes, I remember." She grinned. "That was certainly one of the great love affairs of all time."

"He really fell hard. Did he tell you he went back home and saw her at his high-school reunion?"

"No." She leaned forward across the table and refilled his wineglass. "What happened?"

"She was really fat and had about six kids. She married this guy she met working at the bank."

"Did they have a good time?"

"Yeah. It was strange. Don said it was like they were special friends, like all the hurt had never been there. I guess time makes a difference. But she was really glad to see him, and he was, too. Her husband sounds like an okay guy."

"Bubba, are we going to stay friends? Do you still like me after...I mean, last night?"

He covered her hand with his. "I'm *always* going to like you, Pell-mell. You have my word."

Her throat tightened and stung at his use of her nickname. Her father had christened her Miss Pell-mell because even as a child she'd lived her life at a breakneck pace. It touched her that he remembered.

"I'll even make myself available to take little Bozo to baseball games. I'm sure I can be something of a part-time father figure."

"You'd do that?" She was incredulous.

"Why not? You were a lot of fun as a little kid."

"I remember you used to let me tag along even when Donnie said I had to go home."

"He was always too hard on you."

The wine she'd consumed before, during and after dinner had mellowed her mood. She was relaxed around Bubba again, happy they were still friends. Mel studied Bubba across the table, and her mind began to wander.

She couldn't help but remember what Alicia had told her about Bubba's sexual prowess. Why had her friend even mentioned the fact? But that was Alicia, always blunt.

He filled up her wineglass again, and she realized they were on their second bottle.

"Trying to get me drunk, I see," she teased.

"Of course." There was a look in his smoky blue-gray eyes she couldn't fathom. So she didn't even try.

"I'm glad you came over, Bubba. I would have hated it if we'd become...strange with each other."

"Oh, I don't know." He touched his wineglass to hers. "I think we're kind of strange anyway."

She started to laugh, and a part of her realized she hadn't laughed in a long time. It was so good sitting at her kitchen table with Bubba, laughing at nothing, forgetting her problems.

"You still have that laugh," Bubba remarked.

"It's not exactly something I can just get rid of."

Melanie was slightly self-conscious of the way she laughed. It just seemed to bubble up inside of her until it spilled out. It wasn't exactly a cackle, but it was a good, strong laugh. Bubba used to claim that he knew when she was sitting in a darkened movie theater by listening for her distinctive laugh.

"I'll help you with the dishes," Bubba said abruptly as he pushed away from the table. He seemed a little restless, and Mel frowned.

"No, it's okay."

But he was already clearing the table. "You sit for a while, then we'll go into the living room and listen to some music, okay?"

"Okay." She leaned back in her chair and tried to relax while she continued to watch him. Actually, the wine had soothed her. She closed her eyes and tilted her head back.

It felt so good to have confided her problems to him.

BUBBA DID THE DISHES QUICKLY, concentrating on getting each one clean. He didn't look at Mel, sitting at the table.

When did she suddenly become so good-looking?

It was a hopeless question. He'd already decided, before he came over, that he was going to have no part of what she'd proposed last night.

But it hadn't stopped him from thinking.

She was really pretty in that sundress. Her shoulders were smooth and tan. Her skin was probably soft.

Stop it. He plunged another plate into the soapy water and concentrated on cleaning the dish. He tried to block out his other thoughts.

He'd never noticed how cute she was, how her nose wrinkled up when she laughed. And she was easy to talk to, a good listener.

Bubba rinsed the last dish, then seriously considered sticking his head underneath the faucet.

You're talking about Mel, damn it!

"Bubba, what kind of music do you want to listen to?" Her voice floated in from the living room.

He dried his hands. "Anything." Glancing at the clock, he decided to stay half an hour; then he'd leave.

You just had too much wine. You'll laugh about this in the morning.

When he walked into the living room, Mel was sitting on the sofa. There were two more glasses of wine on the coffee table in front of her couch.

He sat down, placing a little distance between them. "No more for me. I've got to be heading home." She smelled so good, something floral, like her garden.

"Just one more glass." She handed it to him. "It's not like you're driving." She laughed softly, and the sound made him smile. "Anyway, you could always spend the night."

His stomach tightened. It wasn't as if he hadn't before—but as a friend. He'd spent the night on her couch downstairs, once when they'd had a rash of burglaries on their block, and another time when Mel had received a string of obscene phone calls. But something had altered their relationship ever so slightly, and his old sense of being comfortable with Mel was being shaken up. Why, when she'd first suggested he spend the night, did he suddenly picture her bedroom?

He didn't feel like smiling anymore. His hand shook as he took his glass and set it down on the coffee table again. *Clean up your act, now.*

It was as if another part of his consciousness were operating instead of his logical brain. The words were out before he could stop them.

"Mel, have you decided what you're going to do?"

She took a sip of wine, then nodded her head. He liked the way her silvery-blond hair fell over her bare shoulders.

"Alicia's setting me up with a guy tomorrow night. I figure that by the end of a month, it shouldn't be too hard to make sure that—"

He couldn't bear the thought of her with a stranger. "Mel, I've been thinking..."

"About what?"

He knew she didn't have an inkling of what was to come. "I've been thinking I want to help you out."

She stared at him. So he *had* gotten through, after all. Her blue eyes were dark. Questioning.

She set her wineglass down and crossed her arms in front of her. "No, I don't think so. Bubba, I don't think that's a very good idea."

"Don't say no before I outline my plan." *What plan?* Improvising as he went, Bubba explained carefully. "We could consider it a little experiment."

Mel was blushing. She rose slowly to her feet. "Bubba, I *told* you I was crazy last night. I don't even know why I told you—"

He patted the seat beside him. "We'll start slowly. Just one kiss, okay?"

"Bubba, you're crazy!"

"It's less crazy than letting Alicia set you up with some jerk. I've seen the guys she goes out with."

"I'm going to humor you, but only because we've been friends for so long. Bubba, you've kissed me a million times, and I've never felt anything..."

"Sexual?"

She blushed to the roots of her hair. "I was trying to think of a more...delicate word."

"So you have nothing to lose if you already know it's hopeless." He patted the sofa beside him once more. "I just think that in the interest of a scientific experiment we should consider all the angles."

She was laughing now; he could tell she was really nervous.

"Pell-mell, you're ripping my masculine pride to shreds."

She stopped laughing then and looked at his face. "I didn't mean to. It's just....Bubba, when I asked you to get me pregnant, I thought we could just sort of do it quick. You know, go up to my bedroom and turn off the lights, undress in the dark and just kind of get it over with.''

He considered her for just a second before he said quietly, ''Okay.''

''Okay!'' She was incredulous. Then she started to laugh.

''Either you come here or I'm coming over there,'' he said carefully.

''I really don't think this is—''

He stood up and walked over to her. She stopped talking abruptly, and he stood quietly next to her, not wanting to frighten her.

''Mel, let's really give it a try.''

''You're *serious*.''

He nodded. ''Come on.'' Then, without giving her a chance to back down, he grasped her around the waist and lifted her over his shoulder, carefully supporting her.

She bobbed gently against his back as he climbed the stairs, and he could hear her still laughing, with gentle hiccups that made him smile.

He placed her carefully on her bed in the darkened bedroom.

''I can't believe this,'' Mel said softly.

He kicked off his shoes and stretched out beside her, then reached out and pulled her against him.

''Just a kiss, Mel. I'll go real slow. Okay?''

''Okay.'' Her reply was a muffled whisper.

Very slowly, as if he were in a dream, he cupped her face in his hands and lowered his mouth toward hers.

When their lips touched, he felt as if someone were playing with his stomach. The muscles tightened, then he felt a rush of warmth flood his body.

Her skin was as soft as he'd thought it would be. As he smoothed his fingers over her shoulders, he lowered his head again, this time kissing her more deeply.

She responded. Opening her mouth, arching her body slightly against him. When he broke away, her breath came out in a little panting sob. He twined her hair in his fingers and kissed her again.

Oh, my God, it's working. The realization hit him with stunning force. He'd thought he'd have to think of other women, other places.

She was strangely quiet as he held her against him and stroked her back. Her breathing was deep and even. Too even.

Frowning, he levered himself up on the soft mattress.

"Mel?" He turned on the bedside lamp.

She'd passed out.

Boy, that was some kiss, he thought as he began to grin. He'd felt her response as quickly as his own had flooded his body.

So now you're making Mel pass out from the force of your...passion? Passion. What had sparked between them had nothing to do with friendship. His thoughts were humorous, trying to keep feeling at bay. But they persisted in intruding, shaking him.

He smoothed her hair back from her forehead and touched her cheek. Then he smiled down at her face. *Maybe you rushed things.* Maybe this was for the best. For now. He sure as hell wasn't going to let her find some animal out in a singles' bar to use for stud service. Easing her back against the pillows, he took off her sandals, undressed her down to her underwear and turned back the covers. Tucking her in, he lay back and turned off the light.

He wondered just what he would say to her in the morning.

Chapter Three

When she woke up the next morning, Bubba was looking down at her, a slightly embarrassed expression on his face.

She pulled the covers to her chin and looked up at him. He was sitting against the headboard, the covers bunched around his waist.

She studied his eyes and found her own confusion reflected in them. Confusion, embarrassment, even a touch of fear.

Did we do it? Her mouth felt shaky, and she remembered Bubba kissing her, their bodies pressed together on the mattress. Mel looked away and wrinkled her brow, trying to remember.

Why am I undressed? She felt a flush of color washing slowly up her neck and into her face. She didn't remember Bubba taking off her sundress. Maybe she'd blocked out all their lovemaking.

Could it have been that terrible? No, his kiss had been wonderful. Even now, she still felt slightly shocked, as if he'd touched her deep inside.

Did we? She studied Bubba again, willing him to explain. *And if we didn't, is it because you couldn't, didn't find me desirable?* The thoughts disturbed her.

Ask him.

"Bubba?" she asked softly. "We didn't...?"

He shook his head.

Tears filled her eyes, catching her completely by surprise. For some reason, it mattered terribly that he hadn't thought she was desirable. What was wrong with her? First Phillip didn't want to marry her, and now Bubba didn't find her sexually attractive.

"Just let me get my clothes on and I'll—"

"Mel, wait a minute."

She was surprised to see a dull flush creep up his chest, into his cheeks. "I want to apologize. I never meant to rush things."

"Hey, it's okay. I mean, I can't help it if I don't turn you on." Not wanting to prolong this painful conversation, she bunched the covers around her body and stuck her foot out. Her toes touched her sundress, and she curled them into the silky material and began to drag the garment over the carpet and toward the bed.

But before she could pull it underneath the covers and wiggle into it, Bubba surprised her by sliding down into the bed sheets and grabbing both her hands.

"Will you listen to me for just a few minutes?"

The look on his face was so nakedly vulnerable she felt she had no choice. Relaxing her toes, she let her sundress fall on the carpeted floor.

"Mel, you passed out, or...I—I wish we could have succeeded last night. I know you're on a schedule, and if I'd known what was going to happen, I... How would you feel about dating me for a while?''

He's losing his mind. Be gentle.

"Date you?" she replied.

"I know it sounds crazy, but look at it from my point of view. I've known you since you were born. You're the closest thing I've ever had to a little sister. You came over Friday night and asked me to go to bed with you. I didn't really have that much time for advance preparation. I didn't sleep well. I'd been drinking with Joanie. I guess what I'm trying to say is, I want to see you in a more sexual way before I finally make love to you."

She studied his face. *This is insane.*

"I know you're thinking I'm crazy," he rushed on. "But let's set a schedule. You'll be ready again in another month, right?"

She nodded. "Give or take a few days."

He relaxed slightly but didn't lessen his grip on her hands. "So we date for three or four weeks, we get to know each other all over again, and by the end of that time, bingo, you're pregnant."

Strangely enough, she understood what he meant. But she had to ask him a question. "Bubba, if that wasn't, I mean, if you don't see me in a sexual way, what was last night?" She could feel her face flushing bright red.

"Oh, God, Mel, you have to know you're an attractive woman. I enjoyed kissing you, but I couldn't just make love to you while you were out cold. I never would have been able to forgive myself."

She couldn't resist teasing. "But it would have made things so much easier. Then we wouldn't have to date."

She was relieved to see his lips start to curve into a smile. "Don't say that! I'm kind of looking forward to getting to know you all over again."

She didn't answer him right away. It was strangely pleasant, lying in her bed, his warm, masculine body against hers.

He wrapped an arm around her and squeezed her body gently. At that moment, Mel realized she didn't want to be intimate with any other man—just Bubba.

"Okay," she said softly. "We'll try it."

"Great." His energy seemed to return instantaneously. "How do you feel about lunch?"

She smiled. "It's one of my three favorite meals."

He glanced at the clock. "If it's pretty outside, we could take a picnic to Zuma Beach."

"You're on."

Bubba leapt from the bed and tossed her sundress to her. Melanie averted her eyes until she heard him zip up a pair of pants. When she looked up, he was dressed in the jeans he'd worn the night before.

"I'll start breakfast," he announced, then opened the bedroom door. A streak of white fur bounded onto the large bed and rolled over, exposing its stomach to Melanie.

She had to laugh. "Henry, how did you get inside?" Before Bubba had officially adopted the cat, he'd lived at both their houses and eaten double meals. Mel still kept a box of cat food in the cupboard just for Henry's visits. And since her guest bedroom window didn't have a screen, Henry had a tendency to pop in whenever he wanted a meal.

The cat purred as he rubbed his face against her bare arm.

"Go downstairs and let Bubba feed you." She watched, amused, as the cat leapt noisily off the bed and thundered down the stairs.

Picking up her sundress, she pulled it over her head. Date Bubba? How exactly would that work? She'd seen the type of women he liked. And she knew most of his dates were athletic, into outdoor activities. Anyone interested in Bubba would have to be able to hike, swim, bike, play racquetball and volleyball—the list was endless.

No problem there. Growing up in the midst of a large family with two older brothers who were both athletic, Melanie had learned to hold her own at a very early age. She'd never detested physical education in school as so many of her friends had. She'd loved the feeling of stretching her body to its limits. Even now, she worked out with weights and ran early on most mornings. And she'd already played an occasional game of racquetball with Bubba when he didn't have a date.

She sat down on the bed and fastened her sandals. Even if the entire plan went up in smoke, she'd still have time to find someone else. Bubba was only asking her for a month.

It was funny. She would have thought, from the image she'd had of him before, that he'd be ready—physically able—for anything. It was surprising to see that Bubba wanted to wait. To get to know her.

But will he like me when we start dating? The question was tantalizing. Scary. She'd seen Bubba one way for so long; it was going to be hard to readjust her thinking.

She was straightening the bedclothes when Bubba poked his head inside the bedroom door.

Melanie was glad there wasn't as much residual awkwardness between them as she'd feared. One thing about Bubba, she could be honest with him, tell him everything. There wouldn't be any secrets or misunderstandings between them.

"I seem to remember you like blueberry pancakes," he said, tweaking a strand of her hair.

"You? Pancakes?" She was incredulous.

He feigned a hurt expression. "Straight from a mix in your cupboard. Even *I* can't ruin Betty Crocker."

ZUMA BEACH WAS GLORIOUS—clear, hot skies and just a hint of a breeze. Melanie declined Bubba's suggestion that they swim, claiming she wanted to get a little sun and would join him in an hour. She watched him as he walked to the edge of the surf and then began to swim out, paddling expertly as he balanced on his board.

Once he was a dot on her horizon, she lay back on the beach towel and closed her eyes. It felt good, letting the heat penetrate her bones, warm her from the inside out. Being fair-skinned, she'd put on a sunscreen before they'd left, so now she only had to enjoy the weather.

But the intense sunshine had nothing to do with the blush that warmed her cheeks. She could still remember the way it had felt, having Bubba's lips against hers. Her response had surprised her. Melanie had always listened with a tremendous amount of skepticism to stories of being swept away. It had never happened to her.

But last night... Last night had opened up a part of her she'd never had any inkling existed. She wasn't vastly experienced with men, but she wasn't untouched, either. When she'd chosen to be intimate, it had been because of a strong foundation of respect and caring.

But it had never included passion.

Passion. What had Alicia's friend said? *He was the most passionate lover*. It was a strange word to associate with Bubba, but the more Melanie thought about it, the less strange it seemed. He was passionate about a good many things: his surfing, his house-building business, his volleyball competitions, games and sports, their friendship. One of the things she'd always loved about him was that, while Bubba played intensely, he never took sports or games too seriously.

He skims along on the surface. The free spirit again. She wondered why she'd never put the most obvious facts together. If she'd given it any thought at all, it was obvious why Bubba avoided commitment like the plague.

Melanie could remember the one time, when they were growing up, Bubba had asked her over to his house. She'd been in the sixth grade and had been preparing a report about Mexico. Bubba, a high-school senior, had suggested she use the extensive set of encyclopedias in his home.

Later, she'd been positive he'd thought either one or both of his parents would be out. When he'd let her inside his house, closing the door carefully behind them, she'd heard shouting from the kitchen.

Bubba's face had been taut, tense. He'd walked quickly down the hall after asking her to wait in the foyer, and when his parents had returned with him they had been nice, but too nice. Their voices, mannerisms, had been stiff, as if they weren't used to simply talking with each other.

Even as a child, she'd known. She remembered racing through her research quickly, skimming through the various headings in the encyclopedia. Bubba had suggested they take several volumes to the local copy center, where he had carefully made copies of the various pages and then drove her home.

He'd never asked her over again.

She had looked up to him. When Donnie hadn't had the time or patience to listen to what she was concerned about, Bubba had always been there.

Funny how he always knew how to listen when nobody bothered to listen to him, she thought drowsily.

She'd been in the seventh grade when Donnie came home and told the family Bubba's parents were getting a divorce. As she sat at the table and pushed her mashed potatoes around her plate, she thought about how she'd feel if her parents split up.

Donnie had given her Bubba's number at college and she called him. All Melanie had thought about at the time was telling him she was sorry.

Melanie smiled, then rolled over on her beach towel so she could sun her front. What did anyone know in seventh grade? She'd told Bubba he could be *her* brother, since she didn't really care for Donnie, and that he could share *her* family.

He was quiet on the line for almost a minute. She thought he'd hung up before he said softly, "Thanks, Pell-mell. It's good to know you still think about me."

"I always think about you," she said honestly. And she had. Feeling sorry for Bubba that year, she'd written him letters about her various school exploits, sent funny pictures and baked cookies for him under her mother's supervision.

Strange how she'd done all those things for Bubba, never for Donnie.

And it's funny how she could tell Bubba all about her problem, and it never once crossed her mind to call Donnie.

She knew what her brother would say, how horrified he would be if she even *suggested* she become pregnant without the benefit of a marriage license. Donnie was great for doing things one way—his way. And all too often, he still thought of her as his helpless little sister who needed help every single step of the way.

Not this time, Don, she thought, then blinked as she felt a drop of cool water on her stomach.

She opened her eyes, squinting against the bright sunlight. Bubba stood above her, legs spread, grinning down at her. He'd planted his board upright in the sand, and as soon as she opened her eyes he squatted down and sat on the edge of her towel.

"The water's great." He pushed his wet hair out of his eyes. There was one piece that refused to stay, and he pushed at it once more, then let it fall.

"I can give you a haircut when we get back," Melanie offered.

"That bad, huh?" He held out his hand. "Take a walk with me before we eat, okay?"

There was something in his tone that suggested he wanted to talk. Melanie took his hand and he stood up and pulled her to her feet.

She followed where he lead, which was straight to the water's edge. On a Sunday the beach was crowded, and they walked slowly, maneuvering around children and teenagers, surfers, young girls in bikinis, relaxed older people. Melanie waited, convinced that Bubba wanted to start the conversation.

They walked for almost five minutes before he said anything. He held her hand and she was surprised to find she liked the feel of him. His fingers were rough; his hands suggested a man who worked with them. She felt safe with Bubba, and all of a sudden Melanie realized that this was one of the first days since her visit with her doctor that she hadn't thought about her problem in a depressing way.

"It must have been tough right after you found out," Bubba said.

"It was." She liked his matter-of-fact way of bringing her problem out into the open. The few people she'd told had tried to push it away. It was almost as if they'd thought it was catching.

"Why didn't you tell me right from the beginning?"

She chose her words carefully. "I didn't tell *anyone* the first month, Bubba. I just kind of walked around in a daze. I had to think about how I felt about children, whether or not it *did* make a difference. I mean, I didn't rush into having children right away after college, so there was still a part of me that had to decide."

He squeezed her hand and, encouraged, she continued.

"After about a month, I knew it was something I wanted. I always thought there was plenty of time to think about a family, but after I talked with the doctor I realized I didn't have that much. And I thought Phillip was the person I wanted to have children with."

Bubba surprised her by letting go of her hand and sliding his arm around her shoulders. "That guy should have his head examined for dumping you like that."

She had to smile. It was so like Bubba to be prejudiced in her favor. "No, we just didn't want the same things. I can understand it now. I mean, as tough as it was for me to understand, I had to make a big decision quickly. It must have been just as hard for him."

"I guess you're right. But it was hard on you, getting rejected like that."

She was surprised by the words that came out of her mouth. "Not really. In a way, Phillip did me a big favor. It was afterward, when I wasn't as upset as I should have been, that I realized I didn't love him the way I should have."

"You weren't upset?"

"Oh, I was, but only for a few days. Then I just picked myself up and decided I had to get on with things."

Bubba laughed. "You always had a strong streak of independence."

Melanie twined her fingers through Bubba's where they were resting on her upper arm. "Someday, babies and all, I'm going to find a man I really love—the way I *should* love a man—and I'm going to build a life with him."

Bubba was silent.

Thinking he meant to dispute her plan, Melanie spoke quickly. "I know it's unfashionable. I know I'm something of a freak, thinking this way in Los Angeles, but I really do believe in romantic love."

"Eyes meeting across the room and all that?"

"Bubba, don't make fun of me."

He squeezed her shoulder. "I wasn't. You know, I always wanted to experience that, too. I thought, maybe if I met a woman who swept me off my feet, maybe I wouldn't be such a coward."

"You aren't a coward." Melanie was surprised by his revelation. The last thing Bubba was was a coward. The summers he was in college he worked as a lifeguard, and she'd been on the beach once when he saved a young man from drowning. No coward could have done that.

"I think there are a lot of different ways to be afraid, Mel. I don't know what it is, but whenever I start to really fall for someone, I push away."

"Really?"

He grimaced, and she watched as he studied the horizon where the ocean met the sky. "Yeah. Sometimes I disgust myself. The gutless wonder. I mean, Joanie's a great girl to have fun with, but she's no threat to my emotions."

"Bubba, you'll meet someone someday who won't let you push away."

He shook his head. "I doubt it. I make it a practice to avoid those women." His tone was wistful.

She was silent for a moment, not sure how much she could say. She decided she could risk it. "It doesn't have to be the way it was with your parents, Bubba. My mom and dad have been married for thirty-seven years and I know they're still happy."

"I used to love to watch the way they were with each other. I've always been glad I was able to see the good side of marriage and not just my parents'."

"Do you still see them?"

"Yeah. I had dinner with Mom last week. They really are happier apart. I used to feel so damn guilty. I was positive they were together just for my sake. When they got divorced my first year in college, I was sure of it."

They walked along the shore, comfortable in the silence between them, and Melanie thought back to their childhood. No wonder Bubba had been such an outdoors person. Anything was preferable to going home.

"What did you pack in that basket?"

His question made her come back to the present with a start. "Just stuff I picked up from the deli. Sandwiches, chips and some of the lemon cake I baked

Friday." Baking was a passion with Melanie. She liked to surprise her friends with unusual birthday cakes.

"Your lemon cake is pretty good," Bubba said as he expertly turned them around, his arm still circling her shoulder.

They walked briskly along until they sighted his board sticking out of the sand. Right before they reached their towels, Bubba squeezed her shoulder and eased her to a stop.

He turned her in his arms so she was looking up at him.

"So we'll go out for a month and see how it goes. Okay, Mel?"

Something about the way he said it touched her deeply. Her hand reached up, almost with a will of its own, and touched his cheek gently.

"Sounds good to me."

He linked his arm through hers and they walked toward their picnic.

In the month that followed, Melanie never remembered being as busy. Bubba was relentless, planning activities with a vengeance. They surfed, swam, played racquetball and volleyball, and they jogged together every morning. Whenever he went to the gym to work out, he came by and asked if she wanted to go with him.

She began to have him over for dinner at least two times a week. They talked about anything and everything. Both of them loved to reminisce, and they laughed as they remembered so many of the scrapes they'd both come through.

One of the funniest involved the summer Bubba and Donnie "went independent" and decided to move out of their respective homes. It had been a good idea at first, as both teenage boys had been desperate to escape the yoke of parental supervision. But the fun paled fast in light of the fact that neither Bubba nor Donnie knew anything about maintaining a household. Though Mel had been only thirteen to their nineteen, she stopped by their apartment almost every day and brought things she had cooked at home. They fell on her generosity with frantic hunger, sick of their limited repertoire, and finally Bubba broke down and bought a cookbook.

Though Donnie had been indignant at the thought of *really* cooking, Bubba found he enjoyed it, and he and Mel concocted many dishes that summer. Donnie wasn't too proud to eat them. Both Bubba and Mel laughed, remembering all the culinary attempts that went the way of the wastebasket.

She gained an insight into his character that she hadn't had before. Where she had always believed that Bubba had everything in his life in order, she came slowly to see him as a man who held a great deal inside. Not that he was cold. He exuded a boyish, spontaneous warmth that charmed her, made her want to move closer to him, even touch him. But she saw past his surface to the troubled boy he'd been.

While most of his friends were married—with the exception of her brother Donnie, who was just cheap enough to be holding out for the five hundred dollars—Bubba met life head-on and alone. She knew he'd dated a lot of women. He genuinely liked women, and she knew many of his old flames still called him or came over. He seemed to have the ability to smooth the most passionate of relationships into a platonic friendship.

How strange that we're moving the other way, from friendship to passion, she thought one day as she watered the profusion of plants on her balcony. Henry was lying in the shade of an enormous spider plant. Bubba had banished him from the house for tearing open a bag of cat chow all over the kitchen floor.

Their month was almost up. The day before they'd gone to a lawyer and had everything legally drawn up. It had been a shock, seeing Bubba in a suit. She was much more used to him in jeans and sweatshirts. She was sure his mode of dress was one of the reasons he'd decided on construction as a career. Bubba was never happier than when he was outside on a sunny day.

Afterward, he'd taken her out to lunch and had set a date: the Fourth of July. It felt strange to her to plan lovemaking so carefully, but she had to if she wanted a chance to conceive. Usually Bubba had a huge, noisy party to celebrate the holiday; then after everyone had stuffed their faces and played volleyball and lazed in the hot tub, those who were still functioning walked down to the beach to watch the fireworks.

Bubba hadn't extended any invitations this year—except one.

Melanie turned off the hose and rolled it up on the stand, then she walked back up the stairs to her deck and sat down on a chaise. She closed her eyes and let the summer sun wash over her, relaxing her taut muscles.

She felt Henry jump up on the foot of the chaise and slowly walk up her leg, where he curled around on her stomach.

"What does he feed you?" she said as she reached down and scratched the white cat behind his ears. Henry was enormous, nothing like the scrawny, flea-ridden kitten Bubba had found.

The cat was purring loudly, and Mel closed her eyes, content to relax and let her mind wander.

He hadn't even kissed her. In all the time they'd been dating, Bubba hadn't touched her except to assist her in and out of his car or up the walk to her house. He'd been the most perfect gentleman, giving her plenty of notice before each date and planning things he knew she'd enjoy.

I wonder if he's as nervous as I am. Impossible— Bubba, who had had his first girlfriend in the eighth grade? She still remembered the ribbing Donnie had given him about going to the movies with a *girl*. Years later, she'd realized her brother was jealous.

It had been the same in high school. It was a combination of his boyish good looks and his genuine consideration for the opposite sex. Bubba had made quite a life for himself at school, captain of this team, president of that club.

Mel had known all along it was because he really had no reason to go home.

How his mother and father had produced a child like Bubba was beyond her comprehension. She remembered Bubba's mother as a small, pale woman. His father sold insurance, didn't like the outdoors and positively loathed the beach. One summer she'd seen him turning hamburgers on a barbecue grill and had studied his white, sticklike legs, wondering how such a man could have a son like Bubba.

She understood what drove Bubba to open his home to others, to throw such big parties, to date such a succession of women. But what she'd never understood was that, in the midst of all this, Bubba was still lonely.

It was nothing she could put her finger to. Just the way they talked—she had the feeling he didn't have a great deal of experience opening up to other people. She just listened to him, sat quietly on her couch or out by his hot tub and listened. Melanie hated to judge people, perhaps because she'd watched Donnie do so much of it while he was growing up. She simply gathered in what Bubba confided in her, absorbed it and reflected on it. She came away with some very private speculations about Bubba.

The slight creaking of the steps leading up to the deck made her open her eyes and turn around.

"Hi, Bubba."

"I didn't mean to wake you up. I just came over to make sure we were all set for tomorrow."

She admired how calm he was about the whole thing, as if it were some sort of science project. When Mel thought too hard about what had to happen tomorrow, her insides did funny things and her mouth went dry. She didn't want to lose Bubba's friendship. She wasn't sure if she wanted to enter new territory in their relationship. It was all so confusing. Sometimes she just wished she could retreat into her house and go into seclusion for a month, then reappear as if nothing had happened.

But that was impossible.

"All set," she said softly. She studied him. Bubba always looked his best half-naked. He looked most at home in a pair of threadbare cutoffs, nothing else. It was all he had on now. His body was already deeply tanned, but she knew it wasn't anything he consciously worked on.

"I thought you could come over tomorrow night for dinner," he said, studying her expression.

"You don't have to cook for me, Bubba. I can eat something here." Now she was getting nervous, thinking about the weekend.

"It's nothing spectacular. I'm ordering out—Mexican food." Typically Bubba—casual to the end.

"How about something less spicy?" With her luck, she'd get sick.

"Do you like that place down the block with the health-food pizza?" He was making an effort to please her, and she was touched.

"That'd be fine." Whatever he ordered, she knew she probably wouldn't touch it. But she didn't want to take any of the pleasure of planning away from him.

He sat down on the deck chair next to her chaise and stretched out his legs in front of him. She studied him covertly, noticing for the first time the faint network of scars that covered his body. She knew where the scar above his knee had come from—a spill from a dirt bike—and the tiny lines on his chest were cuts and scratches he'd sustained surfing.

"Mel, how are you feeling about this?" His eyes were direct and piercing. Trust Bubba to come straight to the point.

"Fine. I—I just—"

"Are you scared?"

"A little. Not as much of you," she lied easily, not wanting him to know just yet how confused she'd been, "but of the whole idea of having a baby. I mean, it's been an obsession with me. I wake up some mornings thinking I'm doing the wrong thing. Then I think about never having a chance and it tears me up inside."

He was quiet, listening. It was rare that Melanie confided in anyone, but Bubba had always been easy to talk to.

"I don't know what kind of mother I'm going to be. I'm not sure if I'm financially ready. I wish I had a husband, a relationship that had a couple of years behind it."

He nodded his head, urging her on.

"You'll think this is stupid, but the thing that really gets to me is that I'll never have a honeymoon."

"Yes, you will. Not right now, but someday."

"But it's not the same. It's not the same as when you're *beginning* something with someone and everything is stretched in front of you. It's like...I wish I could have done things in the right order."

"You didn't have any choice."

"I know, but it doesn't make me feel any better. I haven't told anyone in my family. You and Alicia are the only two who know. It's not that I'm ashamed of what I'm doing, but I'm not sure how everyone is going to react.'' She sat up on the chaise and swung around, dumping a startled Henry onto the redwood deck. Sitting facing Bubba, she continued her train of thought.

"I feel so...so *vulnerable* right now. I know if I told my family and they looked at me like I was crazy, I might not be able to go through with it.''

"I think you're smart not to tell them.''

Mel sighed. "Donnie will hit the ceiling. There have been so many times I wish I didn't have to rent from him, but he kept telling me I was doing him a favor.''

"You could live in Beverly Hills and own your own home and Don would still want to run your life. You know that,'' Bubba said quietly.

"I know. And Mom is going to look so quietly hurt, I won't be able to stand it! And my father—I think I may just write him a letter.''

"You don't think they'll all understand once you tell them why?'' He sounded as if he didn't quite believe her.

"My family had its moments, too, Bubba. There were certain standards we grew up with, and with Donnie enforcing them, I guess they've been drilled into me pretty thoroughly.''

"But you have to take individual situations into account.''

"I know.'' She sighed, then clasped her hands between her knees. "I know it all so logically, but when I think about telling my family I'm going to be a single mother...''

"Do you want me to talk to Don?''

"No!" She met his gaze directly, fiercely. "I'm telling him last. And I don't *ever* want you to tell him that you're the man who helped me out."

"You're sure?"

"Positive. You don't know what Donnie can be like."

He glanced away from her, over toward his backyard. "Mel, I want you to know something before tomorrow night. If there's ever a moment when you think you might not want to go through with this, I want you to tell me. I don't care when it happens or how far along things go. Just let me know and I'll stop."

Deeply moved by his declaration, she slowly smiled. It was so good talking with Bubba, sharing her worries. It was obvious he cared a great deal about her welfare.

She shook her head. "I don't think I'll be backing out." Even as she said the words, she felt her stomach constrict with tension.

"I'll see you tomorrow night at seven, okay?" He stood up and walked over to where Henry was lying in the sun. The large cat looked up sleepily as Bubba swept him into his arms and chucked him under the chin.

"Okay." Mel watched him until he rounded the corner of her house; then she lay back on the chaise and let out a soft breath.

How was she ever going to get through tomorrow night?

Chapter Four

Melanie stared at the inside of her closet, then turned around and studied the clothing piled on top of her queen-size brass bed.

So what does one wear when one is planning to sleep with one's best friend? Too bad there wasn't an article on this subject in *Cosmopolitan*.

The beginning of a love affair. *Not really.* She wrinkled her nose and began to sort gently through her clothing.

It's not a love affair. He's simply helping you get pregnant.

How clinical.

She hadn't seen Bubba since he left the day before. She knew he was probably getting ready, too, but she couldn't imagine him being as nervous as she was. At least he'd had a considerable amount of practice at this sort of thing.

Well, it's not like you're a virgin.

She tossed a red cotton jumpsuit on the white wicker chair next to her bed.

And it's not like you're Catherine the Great, either.

Preparing for this evening was impossible. There was no way she could do anything with even a semblance of feeling calm. Closing her eyes, she ran her fingers over the clothing on her quilt and grasped one of the outfits.

She opened her eyes as she pulled it out of the pile. It was a dress, a dress Alicia had encouraged her to buy six months ago. One of her favorites, it was a pale blue silk, simply cut. Elegant.

What to wear to a baby's conception. Melanie knew she was being ridiculous, knew her emotions were running away with her. She didn't have any more time and couldn't keep putting off getting ready. She certainly didn't want to be late.

Throwing the dress to the foot of the bed, she stormed into the adjoining bathroom.

If it were possible to boil a body, she did it. Every inch of her skin was meticulously washed, then smoothed with scented lotion. It took her almost an hour to dry her thick, waist-length hair. As she slipped into silk underwear, she caught sight of her reflection in the mirror.

You've gained a little weight. Nothing like anxiety to cause a person to head straight to the refrigerator and stick her head inside. The past month had been a seesaw of emotions—all centered around Bubba.

It's a good thing all your dates were so energetic, otherwise he'd be going to bed with Moby Dick tonight.

She dressed quickly, putting on stockings and heels. So what if she looked ridiculous. This was a big night. Maybe *the* big night. Alicia had an astrologer friend who wanted to do a birth chart based on the time the baby was conceived. Mel didn't know much about astrology, but it was important to her friend, so she had agreed.

When she studied herself in the full-length mirror, sudden panic assailed her. *What am I doing? A silk dress and heels for pizza with Bubba?* Tearing off her clothing, she reached for a pair of jeans and another of her hand-knit sweaters, this time a pink cotton. She applied her makeup quickly, then grabbed her leather shoulder bag and raced down the stairs.

Keep moving, before you have time to think.

BUBBA STOOD LOOKING at his reflection in the bathroom mirror.

Too casual. This is a big night for Mel. Jeans and a sweater just didn't make it.

He strode into his bedroom and began rummaging through his closet. If he'd had his way, it would have been a pair of cutoffs, but he couldn't have Mel thinking this was anything but a serious matter to him, too. So he'd put on a decent pair of jeans and a sweater.

You still look like you're on vacation.

He grimaced.

You might as well wear that hideous Hawaiian shirt Mom brought you back from Maui. Then at least Mel would laugh when she looked at you—break the ice.

He knew she was scared—hell, upset—about tonight. The funny thing was, he'd thought he'd be able to pull this evening off with a minimum of fuss.

Boy did you guess wrong.

He glanced at the bedside clock radio: twenty minutes until zero hour.

Completely unnerved, he began to rummage through his closet again.

SHE HAD TO WIPE her palms against her jeans before she rang the bell. Mel could hear Bubba inside, walking swiftly toward the door. She bit her lip, controlled a purely impulsive instinct to turn and run, and suddenly the door was open.

She stared. Bubba was wearing a suit. It was a beautiful suit, blue-gray and expensively cut. He smelled delicious—some sort of citrusy cologne—and his hair was damp and curly, as if he'd just gotten out of the shower.

He stared at her and she noticed the corners of his eyes starting to crinkle. Then a smile twitched one side of his mouth.

"I don't suppose you'll believe me if I tell you I just got home from the office?" he asked, motioning for her to come inside.

"I know what you wear to work." Seeing him, she felt that everything was all right again. Just for an instant. At least she had a little time before they had to get down to business.

"My mother asked me to lunch?" They were walking down the short hallway to his living room.

"Your mother is out of town."

"I just bought this the other day and I wanted your opinion of it?"

"I've seen that suit before."

He sat down on the couch closest to the fireplace and motioned for her to do the same. "I can't fool you, Mel. I have the fashion sense of a toad."

"That's okay. I only tried on fifteen different outfits this morning."

They stared at each other for a minute, then Mel looked away.

"Why are we acting this way, Bubba? I knew this would ruin our friendship. Why don't we just—"

"Nope. You only have five months left, and sometimes these things take time. I'm sacrificing myself for a higher cause. I knew the job was dangerous when I took it."

He was trying to relax her with humor, and it was working. Laughter bubbled out of her and she leaned back and let the couch support her, feeling much less tense than when she'd rung his doorbell.

"I'm going to run upstairs and slip into something more comfortable. The pizza should be here any minute. There's money in the wallet on the coffee table."

Before she could reply, he'd left the room. She heard him taking the stairs two at a time and she smiled.

Oh, Bubba. What's going to happen to us?

The doorbell pealed softly and Mel took Bubba's wallet off the table and walked quickly toward the door. She paid the teenager, giving him a generous tip, and took the cardboard box into the kitchen. Taking down two plates, she opened the box and pulled out two pieces of the fragrant pie.

Wineglasses were next, and napkins. She knew Bubba was ridiculously proud of his small collection of wine, so she'd let him choose. Closing the pizza box in case Henry was on the prowl, she carried the two plates into the living room.

Her back was to the door when Bubba entered.

"So how do you like the new me?" The tone of his voice was full of repressed laughter.

"Oh, my God." He was wearing his worst pair of cutoffs, faded, bleached almost white, with white denim strings trailing down his muscular legs. And on his chest was the most hideous shirt she'd ever seen, blazing magenta and tangerine. It gave her a headache to look at it.

"Where did you get that?"

He laughed, and she watched as he unbuttoned it. Bubba only half wore most of his shirts. Though he was not overly macho, she knew he liked the feel of a bare chest.

"My mom. If I remember the story correctly, she walked into the store and asked the salesperson for the ugliest shirt in stock."

"And that was it."

"Do you have any doubts?"

She started to laugh. He was beside her in an instant, she felt his arms go around her in a quick hug.

"Relax, Mel. We've got all night ahead of us, and nothing's going to happen if you don't want it to."

"Do you have a camera?" she asked.

"A camera?"

"For when my son asks me where he inherited his exceptional sense of style."

"Funny, Mel." He glanced at the coffee table. "The pizza smells good. Sit tight and I'll get us some wine."

"Let's not get drunk, Bubba." It was important to her, Mel realized, that she remember tonight.

"Not drunk. Just a little relaxed."

He returned with the wineglasses, the napkins and a bottle of burgundy. Opening it with a little flourish, he poured two glasses.

"Here's to you, Mel." Bubba picked up his glass as she did hers, and they touched glasses rim to rim.

"Here's to our friendship." She drank half the glass before she set it down; then she picked up her slice of pizza and took a large bite. She forced herself to chew, then swallow. It settled in her stomach like raw dough. She set the slice down and reached for her wineglass.

"Not hungry?" Bubba asked softly.

"Just nervous."

"Try to eat a little more. It's only seven-thirty. I promise not to start anything before nine."

The smile she tried to give him was so weak her lips trembled. "I'm sorry, Bubba. I'm the one who came to you with this, and I just don't know if I can go through with it."

He set his glass down, the pizza obviously forgotten. "Mel, what will make this easy for you?"

Her face was burning up. Her throat was so tight, she was surprised she could squeak her voice past the constriction. "Remember when I said maybe we could just go upstairs and—"

"In the dark," he finished for her.

She laughed, and it wasn't her usual laugh, full-bodied and rich. It sounded more like a whimper. "Bubba," she whispered, "I wish I were more sophisticated. I wish everything wasn't such a big deal, that I could just *do* things and not think them to death."

"You wouldn't be the Mel I know and love," he said lightly. Taking her hand, he began to stroke the inside of her wrist lightly with his thumb. "You're not going to eat anything if you're this nervous. Why don't we just go on upstairs and see how it goes?"

"Now?" Her cheeks were catching fire again. Why did she have to be so dumb about this?

He cupped her face in his hands. His fingers felt cool against her flushed face. "Mel, nothing that happens upstairs is going to make me think less of you. I don't think you're making a big deal of this. I think you're a woman who doesn't attempt something this important lightly.

She could only stare at him. There was the gentlest, most tender expression on his face.

"I want this to be a good experience for you. Not even the sexual part as much as the emotional part. I'm touched that you asked me, and I want to help you."

She blinked once, twice. Her eyes were stinging.

"Tell me what you want, Mel. Anything." He stroked her cheekbones with the pads of his thumbs, then dropped his hands from her face.

She wasn't giving him back enough. She couldn't let him make all the effort.

"I want to go upstairs. I want to put an end to it, get it over with."

"Okay." He stood up. "Why don't you go up first. You know where the bathroom is. I'll be up in five minutes."

She swallowed, then nodded.

He kissed her forehead, then released her. She could feel his eyes on her as she started up the stairs.

GIVE HER TIME. Bubba carried their plates into the kitchen, where Henry was up on the counter, his paws suspiciously close to the pizza carton.

"No, you don't, sport." The minute Bubba walked into the kitchen, the cat looked up at him with an expression of complete feline guilt in his yellow eyes. He jumped off the counter with a thud and trotted over to his food bowl, meowing plaintively.

"This is your lucky day," Bubba told him as he slid both half-eaten pieces of pizza off the plates and into the pie pan he used for Henry's dish. The cat attacked the pizza at once. Henry loved mozzarella cheese.

Bubba placed the dishes in the sink, then put the carton in the refrigerator. No use tempting fate. Hating to dump good wine down the drain, he eyed the glasses and the two-thirds-full bottle; then he reached up into one of the overhead cupboards and fished around until he unearthed a tray.

Just a little more wine might help her get through this. It didn't take someone with blinding sensitivity to figure out that Mel didn't have a great deal of sexual experience. He knew Donnie had been worse than a Spanish duenna when Mel started dating in high school. When she went away to college, he hadn't been able to grill her boyfriends or intimidate them. Still, there was something reserved, untouched, about Mel. It was in the way she carried herself, the expression he sometimes caught in her eyes.

She hasn't been touched by passion yet. Would it be cruel of him to try and give her that knowledge? Yet he couldn't simply make love to her as if she were a board in his bed. In the past month he'd come to see her as a woman—vulnerable, vital, attractive. On a purely physical level, she had great legs. And her hair—he'd lain in bed nights and dreamed of running his hands through it, tugging it gently as he brought her mouth closer to his.

The sound of Henry crunching the crisp crust brought him out of his erotic thoughts. It had been easier than he'd thought, seeing Mel in a sensual light. She was striking in a natural way, completely without artifice. He'd ached for her when she'd been so embarrassed, so vulnerable, on his couch. Now he knew that she was waiting for him upstairs and that, even though she trusted him, she was still scared.

She was putting so much trust into his hands. Bubba had never had trouble with the opposite sex. He'd always liked women, enjoyed being with them.

But this was Mel.

He glanced at the clock. Five minutes were almost up. Setting the bottle of wine and both glasses on the tray, he picked it up and walked out of the kitchen, toward his bedroom.

WHAT TO DO? Did he expect her to whip off her clothes and climb underneath the sheets? Did he want to undress her? Melanie had climbed the stairs rapidly, then retreated into the bathroom. She'd brushed her teeth carefully, then left the bathroom light on and the door leading to the bedroom open just a crack. She'd taken off her sandals and placed them by her purse near one side of the king-size bed.

Now what? She lay down on the bed, then sat up. The bedspread smelled fresh, as if Bubba had just laundered it. His bedroom was the neatest she'd ever seen it. It touched her that he'd gone to all this trouble for her.

She swung her legs off the bed so she was sitting facing the bathroom door. If only she weren't so tense. If only Phillip hadn't made her feel so inadequate each time he'd tried to make love to her.

He'd rushed her, and perhaps if he hadn't pushed so hard, been so single-minded in his pursuit, she'd have wanted to know him intimately. He'd teased her about being an "ice princess," and she'd merely smiled and lowered her eyes. Yet it had hurt. She'd known he was only trying to make her prove her love for him in the most basic way, but she hadn't felt ready for intimacy with him. Perhaps, subconsciously, she'd sensed he'd never really cared.

It worried her. Was there something wrong with her? Previous experiences had been just that—experiences, nothing earthshaking. She'd enjoyed the cuddling and hugging, but not the actual physical process. There were times, when, alone in her bed and unable to sleep, she'd wished for a grand passion, someone who would sweep her off her feet and make her come alive, make her feel *something*. But it hadn't happened yet. Maybe that was why she'd never been in a hurry to rush into a physical relationship.

She wanted warmth and trust. The men she'd dated wanted physical release. In her heart of hearts, Melanie had always thought of creating children with love, with the sort of passion that existed between two people who cared deeply for each other.

Better with a best friend than some stranger. Bubba was right about that. She'd given a lot of thought to what he was giving up in doing this for her. He would see his child—she had every intention of making sure he had visitation rights if he wanted them—but the baby wouldn't really be his. What would it be like, to have children but not really be involved with them?

She knew Bubba would have never agreed to any of this if he hadn't been sure. Yet she still wondered if she had the right to put him through all this.

The door squeaked gently, and she looked up to see him walking into the bedroom, a tray in his hands. He smiled, and she smiled back, then looked down at the bedspread, suddenly self-conscious.

"I brought you some wine," he said, setting the tray down on the bedside table. "You don't have to drink any of it. I just hate to see a good bottle go to waste."

"Thank you." She picked up one of the glasses and took a sip, just for something to do. *What next?*

"I'll be out in a minute." He walked quietly into the bathroom.

She heard the muted sound of running water. He was brushing his teeth, then washing his face. Melanie fidgeted restlessly on the bed, putting her legs up, then swinging them back over the side of the bed.

When Bubba came back out, he was wearing nothing but his cutoffs. He'd ditched his Hawaiian shirt in the bathroom.

When he noticed her studying him, he said, "I figured colors like that would light up the room, even with the light off."

She nodded her head. There was a pressure in her chest, and she had a queer feeling of light-headedness. Why was her body going completely berserk on her? Why were her emotional responses running riot? Why couldn't she put this entire evening in the proper perspective? She had to get pregnant, and Bubba was helping her out.

Mel had never really learned to rationalize away her emotions; they were always close to the surface.

"Lights-out?" Bubba walked over to the light switch.

She swallowed painfully. *Tell him now.*

"Bubba, there's something..." She clenched the hand behind her hip into a tight fist and rushed on. "I want you to know, if nothing happens on my end, it's not anything you've done. It's me. I've just never really gotten the hang of it. Do you know what I mean?"

She couldn't quite meet his eyes. She felt more naked in front of him than if she'd thrown all her clothes off and paraded around the bedroom.

"Okay, Mel." She felt the mattress depress as he sat down next to her and put his hand on her shoulder. "What I said downstairs still applies. Nothing that happens up here is going to affect my feelings toward you."

She cleared her throat, then continued. "It's just that I know you've had a lot of experience, and you might think that if you took enough time something would happen, but I don't think so. I just...I don't know what's wrong with me. Phillip used to tell me I was cold."

She felt his hand tighten on her shoulder momentarily, but she didn't look up.

"I don't want you worrying about a thing, Mel. Let me take care of it, okay?"

"Okay."

The mattress squeaked again as he got up and turned off the light, then he walked over to the window and drew the curtains. Mel looked everywhere but at him, a part of her still not quite sure how she and Bubba had got here. There was a dreamlike quality to the evening. Reality hadn't set in yet.

He clicked off the bathroom light and the room was plunged into darkness. She heard him go to the door and shut it firmly. Even though the room was dark, she closed her eyes. She could sense his presence in the room, knew a split second before he sat down on the bed next to her.

"Do you want to take off your clothes alone or do you want my help?" he asked.

She appreciated his sensitivity. "I'll do it myself."

She could hear him turning down the bedspread and sheets as she stepped out of her jeans and pulled her sweater over her head. Her hands moved to the fastening of her bra, but her fingers hesitated. Deciding she wanted to have the cover of bed sheets before she took the plunge, Mel lifted up the sheets on her side and slid into bed.

She could hear Bubba sliding in on the other side and she closed her eyes again for one split second. *There's no going back now.*

"Mel? Give me your hand."

She did and felt his firm, warm fingers close around it and gently pull her against him. His other arm came around her shoulders slowly, and then he was easing her against his hard, warm body. He kept pulling her against him until the tips of her silk-covered breasts rested against his chest.

"That's some nice underwear you have on," he whispered softly.

"Thanks."

"I like the way it feels."

Bubba was truly a sensualist. He was the only man she knew who took physical pleasure in an active life. He'd been quite the jock in high school, and Mel knew he was comfortable inside his body.

Well, at least one of us is.

She started slightly as one of his hands ran lightly over her shoulder, then he dug his fingers gently into her tense muscles. He didn't tell her to relax, and she was grateful for that. Bubba simply began to massage her shoulder, slowly working out the kinks. It felt good. Mel began to relax, began to lean into his warmth and accept the touching he offered her.

After several minutes he pressed gently so she rolled over on her stomach. He dug his fingers into both her shoulders, and she took a deep breath. Whatever he was doing, it felt good. He gave her a complete back massage, running his hands over the muscles, releasing some of the tension in her body.

She was barely aware of the moment when his hands moved to the back fastening of her bra, but suddenly her back was bare and he was rubbing it, pressing the heels of his hands against her muscles and giving her firm, long strokes. A soft moan escaped her, and she immediately tensed.

He didn't say anything when he finished, simply lay back down beside her and drew her into his arms. She felt that she was melting; her body felt so pliable, as if she didn't have a will of her own. Mel didn't protest as she felt the silken scrap of her bra slowly removed from her body.

There was a moment of silence. Their faces were close together, so close she could feel the warmth of his breath on her face. She tilted her head back across his arm and it felt good to stretch her neck. Bubba seemed poised on the brink of something. Waiting.

Then she felt him trace the contours of her face gently with a finger, turning her mouth intimately close to his. She knew he was going to kiss her, and she tilted her head closer. She'd kissed Bubba before; this part couldn't be too hard.

But it was a different kiss. His mouth came down over hers, his lips firm and warm. There was the slightest tickle, like the tiniest shock, when they met, and then he opened his mouth to hers as if by that action urging her to do the same.

She was so unprepared for the unexpectedness of the feeling that her mouth did open, slightly, and it was all the invitation he needed. His tongue entered, not forcing its way inside, simply urging her to deepen the kiss. It was tantalizing, the way his mouth moved over hers. He didn't give her everything, but teased, promising more.

She liked it, liked the way he was taking his time, as if they had all night to explore just this one kiss. When his lips finally moved away from hers, she gave a softly startled gasp, then took a deep breath. Somehow, during that kiss, he'd rolled his body so he was positioned slightly above her and to one side. She knew he was looking down on her.

He lowered his head and kissed her again, slowly. He was setting a very gentle pace, waiting for her feelings to catch up to his. It was so different from the way she'd been kissed before. There was none of the mauling quality, none of the scarcely repressed impatience that usually caused her to freeze up inside, knowing she was already behind and would never catch up. But Bubba was urging her, taking her further and further into pure feeling.

The second kiss melted into a third, a fourth, then a fifth. When, in a dim corner of her mind, she realized his hand was finally beginning to move down her body, she tensed in spite of herself. She knew the drill—first one breast, then the other, then down the belly to between the legs, then—

He surprised her, moving his warm fingers slowly down her side to her hip, then rolling her up on her side so their bodies were touching, side by side. Her breasts were bare now; she could feel the hair on his chest rubbing against the tips and for a moment she wanted to press even closer. He didn't hold her tightly, just enough so they were touching. She could feel his arousal, hard and taut against her belly, but he wasn't aggressive. He didn't rub against her or grab her hand and force it down to touch him. It was as if he accepted his body and its responses and wasn't ashamed of what she stirred in him.

Tentatively, she slid her arms up around his neck and pulled his head back down to hers when he broke the next kiss. The feelings vibrating through her were unlike any she'd ever felt before. She opened her mouth a little more, and he was slightly more forceful in his taking. But she enjoyed it, running her fingers through his hair, wanting to touch and be touched.

His hand was moving slowly at the base of her spine, softly kneading the muscles there until she felt that part of her body begin to melt. It was as if her muscles could no longer support her as she rolled slowly onto her back, taking him with her, never breaking the kiss.

When he broke it, she could hear the change in his breathing. It was deeper, more husky. She felt him move; then he was kissing her temples, nuzzling her hair. It was arousing, this slow exploration of her body. No one else had ever wanted to touch her this way.

Tentatively, shyly, she slid her hands from around his neck and touched his shoulders. She *wanted* to touch him, and it surprised her. Usually she felt she had to, wanting to get things over with. But these light, sensual, unhurried touches of Bubba's were different. They made her feel so different.

She felt his muscles tense slightly as her fingers began to explore his back, the powerful muscles, the smooth, hot skin. It *was* easier in the dark, almost as if Bubba had become another person. There was nothing to see, only sensation to feel.

He was kissing her neck, then the spot where her shoulders began, when she surprised herself. Placing the flat of her palms against the top of his shoulders, she pushed gently, wanting to feel his lips against her breasts. He adjusted his position accordingly, and she felt his mouth move softly down the front of her body, kissing, nuzzling, caressing.

When his lips touched her breast, she drew in her breath sharply. Her back arched as if it had a mind of its own. He teased her so gently, so lightly, waiting until he had a physical signal from her before deepening the caress. Melanie had never felt more secure in a man's lovemaking. He was with her, letting her set the pace for what was to come.

Though she had looked toward the final culmination with a quiet dread, knowing she would feel awkward and shy with Bubba in such an intimate situation, this was nothing like she had imagined. It *wasn't* Bubba in bed with her, simply because she'd never seen this side of Bubba before. She'd known of his almost hedonistic pleasure in life, known he liked women, but had had no idea how that would all translate into the bedroom.

He moved to her other breast, and she held his head, pressing against him. Where she had been stiff and clumsy sliding into his bed, now she felt warm and liquid and free, graceful and sensual. Her body seemed attuned to his, wanting more than he was giving her.

As gently as he'd done everything else that evening, Bubba took the lead. He gently removed her last piece of clothing. Mel was slightly surprised when he began to kiss his way down her stomach, but she was still in such a sensual haze that she didn't react until his fingers closed around her inner thighs and he gave her the most intimate kiss of all.

Her eyes flew open at the same moment her hips arched up. A part of her rational mind came to life, intensely embarrassed that Bubba was making love to her this way. She curled her fingers into his hair, determined to tug him back up beside her, but he chose that exact moment to begin flicking his tongue in a most disturbing, erotic way.

Her hands wouldn't obey her. Instead of pulling him away, preserving what little modesty she had left, she feathered her fingertips over his hair, then felt her arms fall away limply to her sides.

Tiny licks of fire shimmered over her body. She felt taut and on the edge, everything within her attuned to what Bubba was doing. He was in control now, his fingers spread over her buttocks, raising her, holding her. And Mel, for the first time, began to feel passion race through her blood. It left her light-headed and weak, almost helpless. As if denying her own sensuality, she felt her head begin to move back and forth on the firm mattress. She bit her lip, clenched her fists, scared of the sensation that continued to build deep within her.

Bubba led her, step by intimate step, until everything was concentrated in the growing heat between her thighs. He was merciless, driving her deeper and deeper, refusing to stop even when he had to be hearing her breathless, throaty cries.

When it happened, she felt as if she were nearing the edge of a waterfall of pure heat and light, caught up in a powerful current that wouldn't let her go. Though for a split second she tried to fight it and swim back the way she'd come, she couldn't. He pushed her over, his sensual caresses causing her to fall over the edge. Everything in her body tightened, then released, sensation ricocheting throughout her.

She felt buffeted by the strong sensations that left her body trembling and weak, barely aware of the feel of Bubba's body as he slid slowly up over her. He claimed her mouth with his, and she could feel the warmth and scent of her arousal. She felt his fingers thread through her hair, holding her mouth against his. These were different kisses again, less arousing, more passioante. Fiercely possessive. His body burned against hers and she welcomed the warmth, the hardness of each muscle. And she was intensely aware of how much he wanted her, the potent proof hard and hot against her.

Everything changed, both of them caught up in that most private, passionate world. This time, when his lips touched her breasts, he suckled strongly, and she recognized the low moans as her own—little sounds of pleading, asking for more.

He was kissing her all over, his hands and lips exploring her entire body. She cried out when he found her center with his fingertips, his accuracy almost heart-stopping in what it did to her. Her thighs drew apart, her legs shaking. This wasn't Bubba, couldn't be Bubba, this passionate man who tore intense feeling from her as if it were due him.

She felt him moving toward the most intimate joining of all, and she moved against him, arching her hips, wanting him to know she was ready, more than ready. Aching for him, wanting him on a purely primal level. It was as if once her awakened passions had been let loose there was no turning back. It was a dangerous knowledge, what her body was capable of, what fire and passion lurked in her thighs, her breasts, even her mouth.

His hands urged her legs apart even farther. She closed her eyes, writhing sensuously against the caresses of his hands. She wanted him, wanted him to complete what he'd started. A part of her thought she would never be satisfied, that he'd never be able to stop her body's desperate, yearning plea for more and more sensation.

She was ready to scream when he delayed their joining, simply lying between her thighs, letting her cradle his hot, aroused body as he kissed her neck. Feeling she was in danger of dying if she didn't know everything about him now, if she didn't have him in the most intimately possible way, she reached down and touched him, closed her fingers around him, urged him toward her.

It was as if she'd released his restraint. He released her fingers, held both her hands in his, straight out from her sides. He raised his hips slightly, then took her in one long, powerful thrust, driving himself deeply inside her. He caught her lips in a kiss, caught the scream before it escaped her mouth, then lay silently, letting her adjust to the feel of him inside her.

She hadn't known it was possible to burn so deeply inside, to feel every part of where he was. Not wanting to wait, she moved her hips against his, strangely satisfied when she heard a supremely masculine groan. And then he was moving, in powerful strokes that seemed to ripple through her entire body. Her hands slid down his back as if each had a will of its own, clasping his buttocks tightly, feeling the muscles move as he did. She felt him pull her hair slightly as he lowered his face to hers, kissing her deeply, intimately.

Nothing was alive to her, nothing mattered except the feel of his body against hers, inside hers. She obeyed his silent commands willingly, wrapping her legs around his waist when his shaking hand eased one of her legs up, arching her hips against his when his fingers dug into her buttocks, meeting each of his thrusts with her own. Nothing existed except him, what he was doing to her, what he was making her feel.

How long he made love to her didn't matter; all that did was that she recognized the resurgence of that feeling again and moved toward it, not away. Never away. Each motion of her body, each time she answered his advance with one of her own, brought her closer to what she wanted most.

When she ceased to think of Bubba, when her body began to respond again with a feeling of tightened anticipation, she heard his breath rasp harshly against her ear. Then his body stiffened slightly and she felt his release. It was all she needed. This time she jumped willingly into sensation, letting it claim total control of her body as it tightly sheathed his.

Minutes later, hours later, all sense of time suspended, she snuggled her cheek against his chest. He lay by her side, his arms warm around her, a safe haven cushioning her, protecting her. She felt his lips move against her ear, kissing her softly. His breath was still coming out in panting gasps; her own seemed to burn into her lungs, as if she'd quickly traveled a long distance.

Didn't you? He had to know what it meant to her, how much he had shown her. Given her. Even if he hadn't given her a child, he'd given her back her body. For now, that was more than enough.

"Thank you, Bubba." The words were barely whispered against his chest, but by the slight tightening of his arms, she knew he'd heard them. She pressed her cheek more firmly against his muscled chest, breathed in the now-familiar scent of him. She kissed his skin, tasted the slightly salty taste, then couldn't move. Every muscle in her body relaxed. Held in his arms, Mel felt herself dropping, falling.

She closed her eyes and slept.

Chapter Five

Bubba woke up with a deep feeling of contentment throughout his body. He wasn't quite sure why, as he drifted in that place between dreams and total awakening. He was dimly aware of a head pillowed on his shoulder, of soft, fragrant hair everywhere.

Slowly, the entire evening began to come back to him.

He opened one eye, glanced down. Mel was curled up next to him, her head snuggled in the crook of his arm. Neither of them had moved last night; both of them had dropped off into the deepest sleep possible.

His arm was starting to fall asleep, but he didn't move it for a second, simply continued to study the face of the woman beside him.

Phillip used to tell me I was cold. His free hand clenched in mute fury. It always amazed him, the men he knew who were so blasé about the emotional damage they inflicted on women. Phillip, the little bastard, had probably said that because Mel hadn't unzipped his pants and knelt and paid homage to him the minute he walked in the door. So she'd carried a load of inadequacy around with her, feeling that *she* was at fault.

What was that bumper sticker he'd seen on the Ventura Freeway the other day? It had made him laugh, coming very close to his own sentiments on the subject. There Are No Frigid Women—Only Inadequate Men. He could understand either a man or a woman not having a whole lot of experience. Even though he had quite a reputation, he hadn't had *that* many sexual partners. Most of his affairs had been long-range, not one-night stands. He didn't really believe there was a great deal of joy for either person that way. After all, if things were good, who wouldn't want to go back for more?

But to *use* someone, to fill another person's emotions full of your own inadequacies simply because someone wouldn't go to bed with you—Phillip had to be one of the lowest forms of vermin to walk the earth.

His arm was hurting now, and he eased it gently out from underneath Mel's head. She looked like a sleeping angel, her long blond hair spread all around her. Her eyes were closed; she was still breathing deeply. Her lips were a soft pink, slightly swollen. But her face was utterly relaxed. Peaceful.

Last night had surprised him. *Correction,* he amended silently. *She surprised you.* He had wanted Mel to enjoy the experience, not have to feel like a mare chained up in a breeding stall.

But you didn't think she'd enjoy herself quite so much. He grinned. She deserved some happiness, after what she'd been through with Phillip. The woman he'd made love to in the dark last night had been a fantastic partner. Warm, willing, sensual, she'd urged him on and on until he'd almost thought he was near collapse.

Even if she hasn't conceived, it was good for her. Hell, it was good for you. It was great.

He slid out of bed as noiselessly as possible. *Let her sleep.* He crossed the bedroom to his dresser and pulled out a navy-blue T-shirt and a pair of athletic shorts. Picking up his running shoes, he opened the bedroom door quietly and stepped out into the hallway, shutting it behind him.

He dressed quickly outside the door, not wanting to take any chances of waking her, and walked carefully down the stairs. As he swung open the kitchen door, the sight that greeted him almost made him burst out laughing.

Henry lay prone on the tile floor, his stomach bulging alarmingly. Small pieces of pizza crust lay strewed across the floor. One yellow feline eye opened lazily; then Henry blinked both eyes and yawned, then stretched.

"So you had a good night, eh, Hen?" He reached into the cupboard and took out the mangled bag of cat chow. If he didn't feed Henry now, no matter how full the cat was, Henry would bound up the stairs and scratch on the door, meowing pitifully. As fat as Henry got, he still acted as if he were starving.

As Henry started to crunch away at his food, Bubba changed the water in his bowl and left the kitchen. He grabbed his house key from the table by the door and let himself out.

MEL DRIFTED AWAKE SLOWLY, not wanting to give up the total relaxation that had swept throughout her body. It was so quiet, so dark, the quilt over her so warm and comforting. Nothing at all like her own bedroom. Her curtains let in more sunlight; she was usually up with the dawn.

She opened her eyes, and as she looked sleepily around the bedroom, she recognized it as Bubba's.

Oh, my God. Now I remember. She could feel her face starting to burn up again. What could he possibly think of her? Like a quickly cut film, images of the night before ran through her mind at lightning speed. Moans, groans, sensuous moves—in the bright light of day, it was embarrassing once again.

She sat up in bed, the covers falling away. He wasn't there. The house was too quiet. Mel combed her fingers through her hair, then reached down for her underwear. It wasn't with her clothing. Blushing again, she stretched her legs and discovered both scraps pushed to the foot of the bed. Donning them quickly, she grabbed her jeans and stood up, then pulled them on. Her sweater was next; then she slipped on her sandals.

She didn't bother with her hair, simply grabbed her purse and started for the door. What to say? What to do? *Thanks, Bubba, for such a swell evening.* She grimaced. It had been so much more than that. How had he reached so effortlessly inside her? It seemed that he'd taken hold of the sensual side of her nature and brought it to the surface. She'd bloomed beneath his touch, found feelings inside herself she'd never experienced before.

You need some time to think about all this. She ran rapidly down the stairs, then to the front door, when a dismaying thought crossed her mind. Gabe was always out in her garden on weekdays, and if she saw Melanie come out of Bubba's front door at this time of morning...

It would practically be on the four o'clock news by the end of the day. She couldn't put Bubba through that. After all, she wasn't really a *girlfriend*. What if he already had someone he cared about? How would she feel? Mel hadn't thought about this before, and now she chewed her bottom lip nervously as she glanced at the front door.

Bubba with a girlfriend: the thought was disquieting. She didn't like the feelings welling up inside her, so she consciously tamped them down and walked over to the sliding glass door in his living room. It overlooked the patio, with its barbecue and hot tub.

She unlocked the door and slid it open, then stepped outside, closing it after her. Crossing his backyard, she threw her purse over the chain-link fence, then clambered up over it and dropped into her side of the yard. Taking her keys out of her purse, she let herself into the house using the back door.

Knowing Bubba wasn't home, she punched out his number on her phone, and his answering machine picked up. She listened to the short message, waited for the beep, then said quickly, "Bubba, it's Mel. I just wanted you to know I left your sliding glass door unlocked, so you have to lock it again." She paused for a second, then raced on, knowing the machine was voice sensitive and would shut off if she didn't keep talking. "I wanted to...thank you for last night. You were...I just... Thank you, Bubba. I'll let you know what happens as soon as I know."

She paused for a second longer. There had to be a way to let him know whether she was pregnant or not without telling him face-to-face. That way, he could make the next move. Because she didn't know whether Bubba was going to want to continue helping her. She rushed on. "If I'm pregnant, I'll run up my rainbow wind sock. If I'm not, I'll run up the green-and-white one." There. That left the next move up to him. He could even think about it for a few days if he wanted to.

"Take care, Bubba, and thanks again."

She hung up the phone, feeling strangely empty inside and wishing she had the right to meet Bubba when he came back from his run, maybe fix some breakfast together, lie out on the patio and talk. But she couldn't. She'd already asked enough of him. The next move had to be left up to Bubba.

Sighing, she settled herself by a window to watch for him. From her vantage point in the second story of her house, she could see his backyard and his front door. She'd make sure Bubba came home before anyone found out his house was unlocked.

She owed him that much, at least.

BUBBA WALKED the last three blocks, letting the deep breaths he was taking calm him. What exactly would he say to Mel? As much as he had claimed last night wouldn't affect their friendship in any way, he was beginning to see her in a completely different light.

His steps quickened. Perhaps if she was still lying in his bed, he could simply lie down next to her and waken her with his kisses. Tell her that he thought maybe they should explore their new relationship. Talk about what had happened between them last night.

He opened the front door, bounded inside and ran up the stairs to his bedroom.

Empty.

The sheets were still tangled, the drapes still drawn. There was nothing left to remind him of Mel except the slightest hint of her perfume on one of the pillows. Or perhaps it was the scent of the shampoo she used.

Bubba was surprised at the sense of disappointment that filled him. He'd looked forward to sharing the day with her. He'd thought about her while he'd jogged, about the two of them lying out on his patio together, then later driving to the market and picking up something to barbecue. And tonight—

She wants a child, not necessarily a man in her life. The thought was sobering. She'd come to him as a last resort, not for anything resembling a permanent relationship.

Call her. He didn't keep a phone anywhere near his bedroom, not liking the invasion of his privacy, so he went downstairs again, to the living room.

The red light was on, signaling messages, so he pushed the button and rewound the tape.

"Bubba, it's Mel." Her voice sounded tentative, unsure. He glanced at his sliding door as she continued talking, then he listened carefully to the rest of her message. A wind sock? Why couldn't she just come over and tell him?

Maybe she's feeling a little strange after last night. It had been a major deviation from their normal relationship. Perhaps she'd woken up uncomfortable with the idea of a friend turned into lover.

He played the message over a second time, listening carefully. That was it. He knew Mel, knew her well enough that he could predict some of her actions. She needed time alone, time to sort out how she felt. It was a momentous decision to have a child. He couldn't forget that her emotions were just as caught up in that as in having made love with him last night.

When the message finished playing, he reset the tape and walked over and locked the sliding door.

The next move has to be up to her. Don't push things—just be there for her if she needs you.

SEVERAL DAYS PASSED, and Mel saw almost nothing of Bubba. Where before she'd thought nothing of running over to borrow anything, from the right kind of screwdriver to a specific seasoning, now she didn't want to bother him.

Something had changed. It had crept up on her without her knowing it, and it saddened her. Some instinct, deep inside, made her sense that there would be no going back. She and Bubba would never totally regain the easygoing friendship they'd shared before.

A part of her was saddened by the fact, but then when she thought about what had happened inside his bedroom that night, how he had awakened her to the knowledge of what her woman's body was exquisitely formed for, she knew she would never want to go backward in time.

Where does that leave us? she wondered, during the times she thought about him. She kept herself busy, knitting more than her usual amount of sweaters, rearranging the store, working extra hours in part because she didn't want to let Alicia down, become less than a working partner. Mel didn't want her pregnancy to interfere with her business or her working friendship with Alicia. She didn't want to stick her friend with all the work, claim that having a child made her unable to contribute.

But most of her busyness was to keep thoughts of Bubba at bay.

Nights were the hardest, knowing he was just a house away as she lay in her bed and played that night over in her mind. Why hadn't Phillip treated her the way Bubba had? If he had, she was sure they'd be married by now and she'd be pregnant. While Phillip had brought out the worst in her, Bubba had pulled out the best.

She'd never thought of herself as a passionate woman, but he'd proved her wrong. She'd been hiding in her own body, refusing to acknowledge something as basic to her nature as the features on her face. So, if she didn't burn in bed, toss and turn and yearn for him—still, she lay awake at nights and wondered what her life would have been like if Bubba had never shown her lovemaking could be different.

She thought, too, about the other women in his life, and realized she had quite a possessive nature. Jealousy crept in slowly, disgusting her. She'd always prided herself on the objectivity of her emotions, but nothing was quite as she'd thought it was whenever her thoughts turned to Bubba.

HE WONDERED if she thought of him.

"You're a damn poor substitute, Henry," Bubba said one night as both of them lay on his king-size bed watching *Romancing the Stone* on his videocassette recorder. Joanie had lent him the tape, claiming that most women wanted to be swept off their feet and he could pick a worse role model than Michael Douglas. He'd laughed, but he was watching it just the same.

"So what do you think, Hen, should I attach a vine to that palm tree outside and swing over to her balcony?"

Henry didn't reply. He was busy playing with a piece of popcorn, batting it between his paws.

"What good are you if you can't give me any advice?" Bubba asked, ruffling the fur between Henry's ears. He was the damnedest animal; he liked being treated like a dog more than a cat. Bubba still remembered telling Mel about that, and she had laughed, claiming that pets reflected the people who owned them.

"And what does that make me?" he asked her, teasing.

"Strange." When she'd seen the mock-hurt expression on his face, she'd laughed again and said, "Individualistic, I meant."

I'd give anything to go back to the way we were. He was having trouble concentrating on the movie. Every time Kathleen Turner looked up at Michael Douglas, he remembered the look in Mel's eyes when he'd walked into the bedroom.

Like hell you would. He'd surprised himself that night. It was as if both of them had shed the protective outer covering they showed the world and exposed the most emotional parts of themselves.

He knew she was embarrassed. In the past, before that night, it was rare to have three days go by without their seeing each other. Now, it had been almost a week and she still hadn't come by.

Maybe letting her make the first move is the wrong idea, he thought. Then he shook his head. He couldn't push her. He had to let her make the decision that was right for her. More than anything, he didn't want to hurt her.

The film was nearing its end, and he watched as Kathleen Turner fought to save herself from the pit of alligators.

"Maybe that's it, Hen. We could ship in an alligator and put you next to it, then when I rush out and save you, Mel would realize—" He stopped talking as he heard the raspy sound of Henry's tongue. The cat had his head stuck inside the almost empty popcorn bowl and was licking up what remained of the butter. There was an occasional crunch as he found a kernel of popcorn.

"A big help you are." He tweaked one of the animal's back paws, and Henry jumped, startled. "Maybe I'd let the gator have you for lunch. It would cut my cat-chow bill down considerably."

Henry stared at him, then lowered his head into the bowl again.

Bubba returned his attention to the movie until it finally ended with both hero and heroine sailing away into the sunset. When the credits rolled, he shut off the set.

Lying back in bed, he closed his eyes.

Why can't real life work out as neatly as the movies?

Because God is not that clever a screenwriter.

He sighed. It surprised him how he missed Mel's head against his shoulders. He hadn't changed his sheets since their night together, enjoying the faint scent of her that still clung to the bed linen. Sometimes, when he closed his eyes, he could almost pretend she was with him.

Wait for the wind sock. She'll let you know how she feels. Give her time.

He wasn't sure whether he was looking forward to seeing a rainbow or a green-and-white banner.

MELANIE WAS WORKING on a new sweater for the boutique, winter-white wool with inserts of angora, when she felt the first cramp. She set the needles down, pressed her hand against her abdomen.

No, please.

But within the hour, the cramping had increased. When she came out of the bathroom, she lay quietly back down on her couch and pulled the knitted peach-and-white afghan up over her shoulders.

She'd taken a painkiller, so she didn't hurt physically, but that didn't stop the tears from slowly forming in her eyes.

Maybe it will never happen for me.

It was a frightening thought. When she'd pictured her future, it had always included children. Though Melanie had been born late in her parents' life and had really been raised by one of her older twin sisters, she never felt unloved. Her mother had given her what she could.

When Mel thought of children, it was with a feeling of what she could give to them. One of the reasons she'd waited was to get on her feet financially. Then there was the little matter of falling in love with a man who desired commitment, no easy feat in Los Angeles, a city that gave the male sex the opportunity to prolong adolescence into their eighties. But if she had to go it alone, at least the boutique was starting to do well. You couldn't rush a business. It took time. It irked her to live under Donnie's roof, but she and her brother had reached a sort of truce, and she didn't see him all that much. She simply sent him her check on the first of each month. Occasionally he'd come by to see her or Bubba—Bubba more often—but he seemed to have realized she was a grown-up person.

But children—she'd been delighted when both her sisters had made her an aunt. She had two nieces and three nephews, and each time she had held them in her arms as babies, she'd anticipated the moment when she would hold a child of her own. It had never been something that had consumed her—just something she knew she wanted to experience.

So you have five months to go.

She wasn't sure if she wanted to ask any more of Bubba. Maybe Alicia was right, maybe finding a man who was a stranger to her was the right thing to do, but as soon as she thought it, her heart rejected the idea.

Feeling totally defeated, she closed her eyes.

BUBBA WAS SITTING in his hot tub when he saw the green-and-white wind sock bob into view. It was windy today, and the colorful nylon snapped in the early-morning breeze.

She's not pregnant.

While a part of him was glad he would have a chance to be close to her for one more night, another part—the larger part—of his emotions concentrated on how he knew she must be feeling. Defeated. Vulnerable. How much self-esteem would any woman possess after Phillip the worm?

He vaulted up out of the tub, splashing chlorinated water all over Henry, who turned tail and darted into the bushes on the border of the patio. As soon as he dried himself off, Bubba pulled on a pair of jeans and a sweatshirt and headed over to Mel's house.

She didn't answer his knock, so he went around back and tried the kitchen door. Nothing.

Not wanting to break down her door—even though that was what he felt like doing—he jogged back over to his house and picked up the phone.

She answered his call on the third ring.

"Hey, Mel, are you all right?"

She didn't respond for a second, and he knew she hadn't thought it was him, hadn't expected him to call that quickly.

She sounded defeated when she answered. "It didn't work, Bubba. Thanks for trying."

"We're not done yet."

"Yes, we are." There was a tired note of finality in her voice. "I asked too much of you the first time. I can't ask you again."

"Ask me." His tone was firm. "Let me make that decision."

"No. I want us to stay friends. If we try again—"

"We'll stay friends. Trust me."

"I do. But I don't...I want you as a friend, Bubba, not a lover."

It was a minute before he realized he was listening to a dial tone.

"I STILL THINK you should consider my dating service," Alicia said the next day at work. Both women were on their hands and knees in the display window, arranging sherbet-colored hand-knit cotton sweaters.

"Ali, I don't have the money right now." It didn't seem like something she wanted to do anyway, pick a father for her prospective child from a television video. It smacked of MTV.

"Then let me set you up with someone I know," Alicia persisted as she arranged the folds of a light lilac-sweater. "You're just about entering your fertile period, anyway, and you didn't do anything about it last month, even with Bubba next door."

Melanie was glad her friend was concentrating on tacking the sweater in place with straight pins and couldn't see the flush she was sure was staining her cheeks. Alicia could be so blunt sometimes. Mel hadn't confided in her close friend about her night with Bubba. It was something she'd wanted to keep private.

"And even if you do go out with this guy, sometimes a woman doesn't conceive the first time."

How well I know, Mel thought as she reached for another sweater.

"Anyway, Joel is gorgeous. He has the darkest eyes, and his mouth is divine. You'd make a beautiful baby with him."

She was glad when the bell on the door tinkled, alerting them that a customer was about to enter the small shop. Melanie had no desire to continue this conversation.

But what was she going to do? She couldn't ask Bubba for any more favors. He'd done enough for her; she couldn't keep imposing on him. Then why was it so hard to imagine making love to another man? It wouldn't be the same as with Bubba, a total give-and-take, an intimate sharing. She'd simply be going through the motions clinically, trying to get pregnant.

She helped the customer, a fortyish brunette with short hair and a slim figure, pick out two sweaters from their summer collection. Mel knew she was a good saleswoman because she didn't pressure. She was also scrupulously honest. If a sweater didn't look good, she was the first to gently suggest another style. She was sensitive to the women who entered her shop, knowing how vulnerable someone was when she was trying on any type of clothing.

When they were finished, she folded the sweaters with tissue and slid them into the silver-and-white shopping bag.

As soon as the woman left, Alicia began again.

"Mel, if you just met Joel, I know you'd like—"

"Set it up." She didn't look at Alicia, knowing her friend would be amazed she'd capitulated so swiftly. She had no choice. It was meeting Joel or choosing to be childless for the rest of her life. So what if she didn't love him? She'd listened to enough of her friend's laments to know that there were a lot of women involved with men they didn't particularly care for.

"Are you serious?" Alicia squeaked, her voice high with excitement. If there was one thing her friend liked more than gossiping about people, it was setting them up. "I'll call him the minute I get home from work, and then I'll call you."

There was no taking her words back now. She forced her voice to remain calm, even though her stomach was doing flip-flops.

"Thanks, Ali. I'd appreciate it."

BUBBA WAS OUT on his patio, lying on the chaise and watching the sun set when the phone rang. When it continued to shrill, he swore softly. He must have forgotten to turn on the machine. Then, realizing it could be Mel, he jackknifed out of his prone position and jogged into the house.

He picked up the receiver midring and answered.

"Bubba? It's me. Alicia."

How Melanie and Alicia were friendly was beyond his comprehension. He supposed they had a lot to talk about, as they were both fashion-design majors and had gone into business together. He'd even gone into their store once, to buy a sweater for his mother's birthday. But the two women were as different as night and day.

"Hi, Alicia. What's up?" He was nice to her for Mel's sake, figuring if Melanie was friends with her, she had to have some redeeming qualities. He just couldn't quite figure out what they were.

"I'm having this party at the end of the month, and I wanted to ask you to come. Nothing fancy, just a barbeque, maybe a swim afterward. Mother will be in Mexico, and she told me I could use her house."

Alicia's parents had money, a lot of which she'd used to open the boutique she and Mel ran. He knew Melanie had taken out a loan for her share.

"Sounds good. Mel and I can drive together." He was trying desperately to figure out something to say to end the conversation. Alicia liked to talk on the phone, and he had the damnedest time getting her to hang up.

This time was no exception. "Bubba, I'm worried about her."

"Oh?" For a split second he wondered if Mel had told her anything about their night together. Alicia had a way of worming things out of people. She was extremely persistent.

"She has this physical problem, and has only five months to get pregnant. And she hasn't done a thing about it."

His lips began to curve upward into a smile. How like Mel, to keep private things private.

"I was surprised she didn't ask you to help her out. I mean, living right next door and all..." her voice trailed away suggestively.

"I think it would be wise if we left that decision in Mel's hands, don't you think?" He was about to terminate the conversation when Alicia's next words caught him totally off guard.

"I don't know how much you know about getting women pregnant, Bubba, but I've set her up with a friend of mine named Joel. I mean, *someone* has to do something, don't you think? Melanie certainly isn't moving on this matter. Anyway, it's a good time for her this weekend, and they're going out to dinner on Friday night. It shouldn't be too hard for her to just let nature take its course. Especially with a man like Joel."

His stomach felt as if it were caving in. "Why are you telling me this, Alicia?"

"I just thought... Look out for her, Bubba. This can't be an easy thing for her."

I'll be damned. So Alicia has depths I didn't suspect.

"She's so...I don't know. I took her to a few bars when she first found out, and even though men are really attracted to her type, she really does need someone to look out for her."

"I'll do my best."

They chatted for a few more minutes, then Bubba ended the conversation as gracefully as he could. After turning on the machine, he stared out the sliding glass door.

It was dusk outside, the twilight deepening into cool evening. Henry had jumped up on the chaise when he'd left it, eager for the warm spot. But he barely saw the cat as his mind raced.

Joel. He sounds just like Phillip. Maybe it's because they both have l's in their names. This didn't sound good. Mel was just too vulnerable, and Bubba had seen one too many of Alicia's friends. As much as she had displayed a quiet compassion for what Mel had to be going through, he knew Alicia's head was still swayed by stupid things: what kind of car a man drove; how much money he made; how he dressed.

You'll just have to think of a way to head this guy off at the pass. He walked back over to the couch in his dark living room and lay down, his hands behind his head. As the beginnings of a plan began to take shape in his mind, he began to smile.

Mel will forgive you. Someday.

Chapter Six

Joel reminded Melanie of Phillip. There was the same quiet touch of masculine arrogance, the same assumption of certain things due him. He took her to a very exclusive, expensively decorated French restaurant and proceeded to order for both of them in fluent French without consulting her.

She had a headache by the time the main entrée was served and merely picked at her food. Mel couldn't get over the strange sensation that one of the things he felt "due" him was herself—spread out on a platter like the poor pigeon he'd ordered for her.

Alicia had been right. He *was* handsome. Dark, with classic good looks, smoldering eyes, a straight, perfect nose and a sensual mouth. The truly unfortunate thing was that he knew it.

Over liqueurs, she debated whether she wanted to ask him in for coffee when he dropped her off. He'd probably expect it. But she'd love to see the look on his face when she simply skipped out of his expensive sports car and said, "It was fun, Joel, but I've really got to run. Let's do lunch, hmm?"

The thought made her smile.

"What are you thinking, lovely lady?"

She almost grimaced at his slightly condescending tone. She wouldn't nurse a broken heart over this man. At least he looked healthy and whole—enough for what she had planned for him.

But she couldn't stop thinking about Bubba.

About all the times she'd gone over to his house to see a movie on cable and they'd ordered a pizza and laughed their way through one ridiculous comedy after another, or the times he'd taken her to the beach and they'd both swum out into the ocean and floated on their backs in the buoyant, salty water. She'd never been afraid of deep water with Bubba at her side.

"About how pleasant this evening has been, Joel," she lied gracefully. Her morals were going straight to hell. After tonight's mission was accomplished, she'd have to straighten out and fly right.

He seemed pleased. His dark eyes glowed with barely concealed admiration as they swept over her. She'd worn her hair up, pinning it with several strategically placed combs. Alicia had helped her pick out a dress over the phone and she had settled for the classic light blue silk. She couldn't help remembering the last time she'd put it on—that night with Bubba. She hadn't felt comfortable in it then and she certainly didn't feel comfortable in it now. She was more herself in a bikini, running along the shoreline and laughing with Bubba.

Why can't you stop thinking about him? You made your decision; now live with it.

Joel approved of her, she could tell. He would think the same way Phillip had—that she was there for his pleasure. That she was beautiful would only whet his appetite, but Mel already had a secret emotional plan. She wouldn't respond. She would keep that small part of herself whole, never to be violated by the likes of him.

He probably won't even notice.

Joel signaled for the waiter, paid the check with a major snob credit card and assisted her into the expensive jacket Alicia had lent her. They walked outside into the balmy August night air, and he spoke softly with the parking attendant. When the red Porsche pulled up, he helped Melanie into the passenger seat, his hand lingering on her elbow for just a second more than was necessary.

She stared out the front windshield, forcing herself to remain calm even though inside she felt she was dying.

He slid into the driver's seat and started up the engine. It purred softly. It even sounded expensive.

"Your place or mine?" he asked, one dark brow slanting up.

Mother of God. "Mine." She clasped her hands together tightly in her lap and spoke quickly before she could back down. "Would you like to come in for coffee?"

The slightly smug look on his chiseled features made her want to punch him, if only to ruffle the perfect symmetry.

"I'd like that. Very much."

Why do I get the feeling this guy has said the same thing a thousand times, with the same inflection? But

Alicia had been right. He was handsome and he would do the job.

Miserable, she stared out the window as he turned out of the driveway and headed back toward her house.

"THEY'RE LEAVING the restaurant now, Bubba, and heading toward Mel's."

"You're sure?" Thank God for his best buddy, Terry. Thank God for car phones and thank God they weren't going back to Joel the worm's bachelor pad.

"I'm right behind them. They're on their way."

"Terry, if anything happens, if they go anywhere else, just follow them and when they get outside the car, grab Mel."

"Don't worry, Bubba. They're turning west on Wilshire right now. Joel lives in the other direction."

"Thanks, Terry. I'll be leaving the house now, and I owe you one." He could just picture Terry's smile; the amusement sparkling in his green eyes. He'd met him in college, and when Terry had broken up with his wife, he'd come out West. Bubba had given him a job, helped him get back on his feet both financially and emotionally. If there was one man he could trust, it was Terry.

"Good luck, old buddy."

He smiled and hung up the phone. Henry was sitting next to the phone on the end table, stretched out underneath the heat and light of the lamp.

"I've left you plenty of food, Hen. Don't worry about me, boy. I'll be back on Monday." He gave the cat an affectionate pat, and Henry swiped at his fingertips with his paws, held them, then gently bit them.

"Same to you, whatever that means in felinese."

He didn't have any time to spare. For once, his athletic training was going to come in handy. Locking the back door behind him, he ran to the fence separating his and Mel's backyard and scaled the chain links easily. Dropping down into her garden, he tried not to smash too many of her flowers.

The rest was ridiculously easy. He had a set of keys to the house. Donnie had insisted on that, in case there was an emergency. Though Bubba didn't approve of the tight rein Mel's older brother held over her, in this case Donnie's stubbornness had come in handy.

He opened the back door with ease, then locked it behind him. Mel had left one light in the living room on and one upstairs in her bedroom. He made his way to the dining room, just off the living room. Then he sat down, his body hidden from view by the dining-room table.

They'll be here any minute. He hoped they were really coming there. He'd hate to think of the tongue-lashing he'd receive from Mel if Terry had to "kidnap" her.

With a sudden flash of inspiration, he got up and raced to her refrigerator. Quickly pulling out bologna and bread, he made himself a sandwich. Then he grabbed an apple out of the bowl on the counter, put the rest of the meat and bread away in the refrigerator and grabbed a can of grape soda.

Stalking back into the dining room, he sat down against one of the table legs and waited.

"WELL, HERE WE ARE." Mel knew she was babbling, but she was so nervous. Her instincts were screaming that this was a big mistake. Part of her, the very practical, stubborn aspect of her personality, knew she had to go through with it anyway.

Joel raced around to her side of the sports car to help her out, but she was already shutting the door. To hell with him. She just wanted the evening over. Why play games? It was obvious they'd never see each other after tonight. She was sure she didn't want to.

Her hands shook as she opened the door. Joel had made a move to take her key from her, do it for her, but she clung stubbornly to the last vestiges of her independence.

Just pretend he's Bubba.

"You have such a charming home."

And you aren't an Academy Award—winning actress. Just get it over with.

She supposed she ought to make a show of making coffee for him, but Joel solved the problem for her.

"Come here, princess."

Princess! God, what do these guys do, go to the same finishing school? She gritted her teeth, forced a smile and walked straight into his arms.

He kissed her, and his caresses left her totally cold. Mel was surprised to find that, despite the show of confidence Joel had exuded, he wasn't much in the way of a kisser.

She started when she felt something soft and hairy twine around her legs.

Joel broke the kiss. "What the—"

Mel glanced down and had to smile. Henry was weaving around their legs, leaving a tremendous amount of white cat hair all over Joel's impeccable suit pants.

"Henry, what are you doing here?"

Henry! Bubba swore softly as he started to get up, but he bumped his head on the side of the dining-room table before he realized his presence was supposed to be a secret. For now anyway.

That damn cat. He must have smelled the bologna.

"Henry! Hen!" He could hear Mel's voice. She was coming closer. Henry darted into the dining room, and Bubba grabbed him by the leg as he skidded past.

The cat started to yowl, but Bubba put his hand over its mouth and Henry bit him instead.

"Don't go after that hairy little beast, Melanie. He's gone now. Let's relax."

There was a moment of silence. Then Mel said softly, "All right."

Bubba slowly removed his hand from Henry's mouth. With the inspiration that comes from desperation, he put half the bologna sandwich in front of Henry's face.

The cat picked up a corner of the sandwich and proceeded to drag it into the kitchen.

Bubba sighed with relief. He knew Mel kept a bowl for Henry in her kitchen, and Henry had a thing about eating out of bowls. That half a sandwich would occupy him for the next fifteen minutes, and that was all the time Bubba needed.

Maybe I could throw the cat on top of him....

"You are so exquisite, Melanie." Joel's voice floated into the dining room. "Take down your hair for me. I want to see the real you, that golden mane down around your shoulders."

I'm going to throw up. Bubba glanced at his watch. Maybe it would only take five minutes. The thought of this creep's hands on Mel was enough to give him cardiac arrest.

There was too much silence from the living room. The lights were too low. Sandwich, apple, and soda can in hand, Bubba began to inch to the doorway. He had to be careful. He didn't want either of them to see him. Not yet.

There were folding doors between the dining room and living room, the panels like shutters. Bubba crawled up behind one of them and, holding his breath, moved the slats ever so gently—just enough to give him the view he wanted.

They were on the couch. Mel's hair was down and Joel was running his hands through it and kissing her at the same time. She didn't seem to be having such a good time, and Bubba was suddenly fiercely glad he'd thought up his plan.

"Kiss me, Melanie, like you really mean it."

Where did this guy get his dialogue? He couldn't have been watching the same cable movies he and Mel enjoyed. Maybe he read badly written novels, or maybe he was one of those guys who ordered the books in back of men's magazines: *One Thousand and One Opening Lines* or *Girls! Girls! Girls!* Either way, this guy's performance was *not* very impressive.

Bubba waited in the shadows until Joel made his first big move, pressing Mel down into the depths of the sofa and climbing on top of her.

He's not much for the subtle approach. Bubba found that his jaw was aching with the effort to keep himself from crying out. He couldn't stand to see her violated. How would she ever be able to raise the child, remembering this creep?

His bare feet making no sound over the plush carpet, Bubba glided slowly toward the chair on the edge of the living room and sank into it. He set the apple down on the small table next to the chair and took a bite out of his sandwich. Even though it felt like clay in his throat, he forced himself to chew and swallow.

He'd give the bastard *exactly* thirty seconds before putting his plan into effect.

MEL KEPT HER EYES SHUT as Joel lowered her to the couch. His hands were making quick forays down her sides, and she knew any minute he would zoom in on her breasts. He had the subtlety of a tomcat and just about as much finesse.

Why did she keep thinking about Bubba? Each time Joel kissed her, touched her, her mind kept flashing back to the night she'd spent in Bubba's arms. He'd taken so much time with her, urged her along slowly. With Joel, it was exactly as it had been with Phillip. He didn't give; he took, taking his own pleasure selfishly. She could have been one of those rubber dolls advertised in the back of men's magazines for all she meant to him.

It's wrong. It's the wrong way to conceive a child, and you know it. Though Joel would be furious with her, she had to stop him. She couldn't do this to herself, no matter how badly she wanted a baby.

And why do I have the strangest sensation—almost as if Bubba knows exactly what's happening to me? They were extremely close but had never been psychic. She opened her eyes as Joel's hand mashed her breast, and then drew in a sharp breath.

Bubba knew exactly what was happening to her because he sat not more than fifteen feet away, chewing on a sandwich and calmly watching. When her body went rigid, Joel raised his head.

"Melanie, loosen up. How am I supposed to enjoy this if you—" He stopped talking as he noticed the direction of her gaze, then he looked over her shoulder and saw Bubba.

Joel levered himself up off her in a flash, adjusting his pants and tucking in his crisp white evening shirt. "What is the meaning of this!"

Bubba waved what was left of his sandwich in the air in a supremely casual gesture. "You two just go right ahead. Don't let me bother you."

"Who *are* you, and just what are you doing in that chair?" Joel demanded furiously.

Bubba popped open a can of soda and took a long swallow.

Joel turned furious eyes on Melanie. "Who is this man!"

"He's my...he's my neigh—" To her horror, she couldn't make the words come out of her mouth. She was torn between a desire to laugh and cry, or maybe she'd do both.

"I'm her husband." Bubba put the soda can down on the end table and burped softly. "Melanie humors me sometimes by bringing home different men." He smiled at Joel as if they were discussing batting averages. "I'm sure you get my drift."

Melanie watched, fascinated, as a muscle in Joel's jaw began to work furiously. She'd only read about that in books. She'd never really seen it. Her desire to laugh was steadily winning out over her impulse to cry.

"Speechless?" Bubba took a huge, crunching bite out of his apple, chewed it, then swallowed. "You shouldn't be, not a man of your obviously sophisticated tastes."

"You should have told me!" Joel said, his dark gaze on her, furious.

Mel shrugged. "Most guys don't seem to care."

"Now both of you settle down and make believe I'm not here." Bubba took another noisy bite out of his apple. As if on cue, Henry sauntered into the living room and jumped into his lap, affectinately nuzzling the hand that held the apple.

"You're sick!" Joel exploded, turning on Melanie. "Alicia didn't tell me anything about this or I would never have asked you out!"

Mel was beginning to enjoy herself. "But Alicia told me you were a pretty wild and crazy guy." She put her arm around his neck, tried to pull his head against hers. "Anyway, it's easy. Like Bubba said, just pretend he isn't there."

"Mel's right. Just don't even look at Henry and me and we'll all be happy as—"

"How can you live with a...a..." Joel was sputtering now, his face a dull shade of red.

"A pervert like me?" Bubba supplied cheerily. "You've got to understand something pretty basic to Mel's personality, Raoul."

"The name is *Joel*," he said through gritted teeth.

"Like I said, Joe, the thing you've got to understand is that, well, basically Mel is one hell of a good sport."

"You're both *sick*! *Sick!*" Joel got up swiftly off the couch and grabbed his suit jacket. He stormed toward the door and fumbled with the lock.

"Hey, Noel, thanks for taking Mel out to dinner. I don't really care that much for French food."

His answer was the sound of a door slamming.

They were silent as they heard the sound of a revving engine, then the squeal of burning rubber as the Porsche shot out of the driveway.

After another moment of silence, Bubba offered Mel his can of soda.

"Do you want some, to get rid of the aftertaste?"

She sighed. "I was going to ask him to leave. I knew it wasn't working."

"Just consider what I did as a favor."

She looked away from him, her hair swinging over to cover the side of her face closest to him.

"Okay, Mel, what are you thinking?"

"I just...I'm back to square one again."

"I wouldn't say that." He picked Henry up and set him down gently on the carpet.

She stared at him. "Bubba, we've had this discussion before. You know how I feel about this,"

"I do." He got up from his chair and walked over to her. "You made yourself very clear." He stood looking down at her.

"So you can see why—"

"I can see why I'm going to have to take this particular decision out of your hands." With one swift movement he swung her up over his shoulder and began to walk toward the stairs.

"This is not funny. Put me down."

He swatted her fanny lightly. "Better me than Raoul. At least I fix you breakfast once in a while."

"Bubba, I don't want—"

"I don't want you sleeping with some idiot just to produce a child. My God, what would you have done with Noel's child? He probably would have demanded nouvelle cuisine the moment he popped out."

Despite her firm resolve, she started to laugh. He set her down on the bedroom floor and crossed his arms in front of his chest.

"Okay. You've got me, Mel. Now you can have your wicked way with me."

"Oh, please, Bubba. Lock the door when you leave."

She turned, kicked off her heels, picked them up and began walking toward her closet. When she felt strong arms encircle her waist, she let out a sharp gasp of protest. Before she knew what was happening, Bubba had her gently pinned to her mattress, his body warm and hard against hers.

"I'm not going to ask again nicely." He kissed her cheek and she squirmed beneath him. "Now, I happen to know you're fertile as a turtle this weekend, so I'm going to take it from there."

"Who told you?"

"I have my methods. Now are you going to take your clothes off or am I going to have to ravish you?"

He's doing this to be nice to you. To make up for Joel. She couldn't let Bubba father a child out of sympathy for her. That would be as wrong as that fiasco on the couch earlier.

It's more than that and you know it. You care for him. You— She stopped her train of thought before it progressed any further.

You're afraid. Afraid of the way he makes you feel. Afraid because no other man has ever made you feel so deeply and completely vulnerable.

She must have had doubt in her eyes, because his facial expression slowly changed as he looked down at her. His eyes softened and concern etched his face.

"Mel? Is something wrong?"

When she didn't answer, he said softly, "I'm sorry. If you really don't want me to—"

She had to tell him the truth. Putting a finger across his lips, she whispered, "It's just that sometimes I'm afraid."

"Afraid? Of me? Why?" He was genuinely incredulous.

"Afraid of the way you make me feel." There. She'd said it. It was out in the open now.

"I'm going to let you in on a big secret, Mel." He lowered his head and softly kissed her ear. "It works both ways."

"Really?"

"Yeah."

"Really?"

"Do you want a signed confession or what?"

She smiled slowly, her eyes never leaving his face. A deep satisfaction, a certainty that she was doing the right thing, filled her. Bubba was the man who would father her child. "I'll take my clothes off now."

He got off the bed, then drew her to her feet. "Now that's the type of bedroom talk I like to hear."

She reached in the back for the zipper of her dress.

"Let me."

The cool air hit her skin as Bubba slowly lowered the zipper, kissing her skin as he bared it to his touch.

"You smell good."

"It's French perfume."

"You wasted something like that on a jerk like—"

She turned in his arms and put her finger to his lips again. "I don't ever want his name mentioned in this house."

"You've got a deal."

He undressed her slowly, teasing, caressing. When he unfastened her lacy bra, Mel glanced over at the bedside lamp. "Bubba, couldn't we—"

"I want to see you this time. Please, Mel."

She lowered her eyes to the carpet, slowly slid her bra straps over her bare arms, then dropped the lacy garment on the carpet.

"Come here, gorgeous." He caught her hand, pulled her against him and started to kiss her.

His touch seemed to burn away Joel's, and she welcomed the feeling. As he kissed her, Bubba walked her slowly toward the bed until she felt the back of her knees against the mattress. He eased her down onto it, then covered her body with the warmth of his own.

He had most of his clothing off when the phone shrilled angrily.

Mel struggled up, convinced that Joel had called Alicia and that her friend was trying to reach her for an explanation. "Bubba, I—"

He covered her mouth with a kiss, at the same time reaching for the phone cord and yanking the jack out of the wall.

MUCH LATER IN THE EVENING, his arms wrapped snuggly around Mel's soft body, Bubba smiled contentedly. It was early Saturday morning, and he didn't plan on returning home until Monday. If things went as he'd planned, Mel would get pregnant that weekend.

After they'd made love, he'd turned off the light. Her bedroom was like a warm, dark cocoon, their own private, sensual world.

"Raoul." Her voice came out a soft whisper, then she started to laugh the laugh he loved. It seemed to come straight out of her body, starting at her toes. He felt her turn her mouth against his chest to stifle the sound. "Oh, Bubba, how could you?"

"It was him or me," he said, his voice gravelly with mock exhaustion. "I had to fight dirty."

"The look on his face when you waved that sandwich."

"Pretty inspired." He kissed her forehead.

"What would you have done—" she started to laugh again "—what would you have done if he'd said okay?"

He smiled. "I'd have brought out my secret weapon. I would have insisted Henry join in."

She shrieked with laughter, burying her face in the pillow. He rolled over onto his side, taking her into his arms and hugging her against his body. When she stopped laughing, he kissed her softly on the mouth.

"Now get some sleep. I've got the alarm set for ten."

"Don't you want to sleep in? It's Saturday."

"I plan on waking you up and ravishing you. We're on a schedule this weekend, Mel. These things take careful planning. You can't leave anything to chance."

She was laughing again.

"You didn't make any other plans for this weekend, did you?"

"No, just Raoul."

"You're booked solid now. Stop laughing and get some sleep. I have great plans for you."

She snuggled against him, tucking her head underneath his chin and sighing contentedly.

"Good night, Raoul."

He pinched her bottom and she yelped.

Chapter Seven

"So you and Joel didn't hit it off, huh?" Alicia was busily folding sweaters and rearranging them in an oak-and-glass display case near the register.

"Did he tell you that?" Mel couldn't imagine Joel telling *anyone* the truth about what had happened that night.

"No. He just said you weren't quite what he expected."

Mel bit her lip and turned on the vacuum. It was Monday morning. Bubba had gone before she woke up, but he'd left a note on the pillow: "I expect to see a rainbow next time. Bubba."

It was twenty minutes before they normally opened the shop. Alicia had brought in croissants and two coffees, but Mel had explained she'd already had breakfast: poached egg, a piece of fruit and a slice of whole-grain bread. She'd decided not to take any chances, just in case.

After Mel finished vacuuming, Alicia started in again.

"So there's this guy I know, Fred, who'd be just perfect."

"I don't need anyone."

"Mel, we have to start thinking ahead. Time is running out and—"

"I found someone else." This wasn't totally a lie.

"Who?"

Mel had no qualms about lying this time. She didn't want Alicia calling Bubba, making a pest of herself. She also didn't want to talk about him constantly with her, even if she was a good friend. And she wanted to respect Bubba's privacy.

"I went out Saturday night. To a party."

"Whose house? Where? Do I know him?"

She shook her head. "Friends of my sisters. Anyway, there was this very sweet man there, and I explained my predicament to him. He was glad to help me out."

"That's terrific! Does he live around here?"

"Nope. He left Sunday." She thought quickly. "He lives in Alaska; he's working on the pipeline." That ought to discourage even Alicia.

Her friend looked so discouraged for a moment that Mel almost walked over and gave her a quick hug. Alicia loved intrigue among people she knew. If she'd had a different type of personality, Mel might have considered confiding in her. But it was simply not to be.

"Did you get his address? I mean, will you send him pictures of the baby when it's born? Does he want to know whether he has a son or a daughter?"

"He's married."

"Oh, Mel!" Alicia looked horrified, but Mel knew she loved hearing every minute detail. "How awful for you!"

"Not really. I mean, I knew exactly what I was getting into to begin with."

"But to never see him again, to always wonder..."

"It's okay, Ali. He was really nice about it. Anyway, I'm sure I'll marry someday. There are plenty of women with children from a first marriage who get married a second time."

"You're braver than I am."

Alicia seemed content with Mel's story, and the two women continued working, cleaning and setting up displays. Mondays usually weren't busy, and Mel was thankful. She needed the time to sort out her tumbled emotions.

During quiet moments that day, Mel thought back over the weekend. She and Bubba had rarely left her bedroom. If she'd thought the first time they made love had been fulfilling, the weekend had surpassed her wildest imaginings. Bubba had so many moods as a lover: tender and quietly erotic, demanding, playful, inventive. She'd learned there was so much more going on inside him, right below the surface.

She'd carefully resisted pinning any hopes on the weekend. Bubba was acting as a good friend—nothing more. For her to think of any other kind of commitment would lead to the end of their friendship. He was a man who played by his own rules, as unorthodox as they were. It was enough that he had helped her twice, not let her be mauled by Joel and agreed to take some part in raising the child.

Would it really be any different than if they'd married and divorced? Most women she knew took sole responsibility for child care in the early years, with fathers only beginning to chip in as the children became more and more independent. Bubba would be her child's natural father—but still a surrogate. He would fill the void nicely and provide a masculine influence.

Don't plan too far ahead. You don't even know if you're pregnant.

The bell on the door tinkled sweetly, and she looked up, ready to smile.

BUBBA STOOD under the hot shower, letting the water work the stiffness out of his muscles. He'd been working double shifts for the past three days. There were too many things that had to be done and not enough time.

He leaned back into the hot spray, sighing as the stinging water began to work out the knots in his back.

Mel. He hadn't known what to say Monday morning. It had been an incredible weekend—and not just sexually. He'd never felt closer to another human being. Actually, he'd always felt close to Mel, but until now, there hadn't been a sexual element to their relationship.

And there probably never would have if she hadn't been desperate. The whole thing confused him. Eight weeks ago, a serious relationship would have been the furthest thing from his mind. Now, he was contemplating one.

GIVE YOUR HEART TO HARLEQUIN®

FREE!

Mail this heart today!

❧ IT'S A ❧
HARLEQUIN HONEYMOON
A SWEETHEART
OF A FREE OFFER!

FOUR NEW "HARLEQUIN AMERICAN ROMANCES"—FREE! Take a "Harlequin Honeymoon" with four exciting romances—yours FREE from Harlequin Reader Service. Each of these hot-off-the-presses novels brings you all the passion and tenderness of today's greatest love stories...your free passports to bright new worlds of love and foreign adventure!

But wait...there's <u>even more</u> to this great offer!

HARLEQUIN PEN AND WATCH SET—ABSOLUTELY FREE! You'll love your personal Harlequin Pen and Watch Set. Perfect for daytime...elegant enough for evening. The watch has a genuine leather strap and replaceable battery. The watch and the stylish matching pen are yours free with this offer!

SPECIAL EXTRAS—FREE! You'll get our free monthly newsletter, packed with news on your favorite writers, upcoming books, and more. Four times a year, you'll receive our members' magazine, Harlequin Romance Digest! <u>Best of all,</u> you'll periodically <u>receive our special-edition "Harlequin Bestsellers," yours to preview for ten days without charge!</u>

MONEY-SAVING HOME DELIVERY! Join Harlequin Reader Service and enjoy the <u>convenience</u> of previewing four new books every month, delivered right to your home. Each book is yours for only $2.25—25¢ <u>less per book</u> than what you pay in stores! Great savings plus total convenience add up to a sweetheart of a deal for y<u>ou</u>!

ARC/U 8/85

START YOUR HARLEQUIN HONEYMOON TODAY—
JUST COMPLETE, DETACH & MAIL YOUR FREE OFFER CARD!

HARLEQUIN READER SERVICE

◦§ FREE OFFER CARD ?◦

PLACE HEART STICKER HERE

FREE
PEN AND
WATCH SET

FREE
HOME
DELIVERY

PLUS AN
EXTRA BONUS
"MYSTERY
GIFT"!

4 FREE
BOOKS

☐ **YES!** Please send me my four HARLEQUIN AMERICAN ROMANCES™ books, <u>free</u>, along with my <u>free Pen and Watch Set</u> and <u>Mystery Gift</u>! Then send me four new HARLEQUIN AMERICAN ROMANCES books every month, as they come off the presses, and bill me at just $2.25 per book (25¢ less than retail), with no extra charges for shipping and handling. If I am not completely satisfied, I may return a shipment and cancel at any time. <u>The free books, Pen, Watch and Mystery Gift remain mine to keep!</u>

FIRST NAME_____ LAST NAME_____
                              (PLEASE PRINT)

ADDRESS_____ APT._____

CITY_____

PROV./STATE_____ POSTAL CODE/ZIP_____

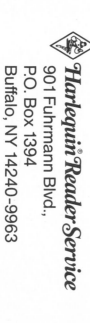

But the craziest thing was that he still wasn't sure about marriage. And fatherhood? That was a whole other ball game.

He stepped out of the shower, knotting a towel around his waist and taking down another to dry his hair. He hadn't been consciously avoiding Mel; it was just that his business demanded his attention. It was an emotionally loaded issue, his success. His father had wanted him to sell insurance, but being confined behind a desk day after day had seemed to him like walking straight into a living death and the very thought of it repelled him.

So he'd started working on construction jobs right out of college. He'd taken a business degree, thinking that there might be some way he could combine his love of the outdoors with a successful career. If he was making good money, then even his father couldn't get to him.

He and his father had never been close. Bubba had always sensed a distance. Nothing was ever said, but he'd felt it, even as a small child.

So he had worked hard, watched and learned. He never had to be told something twice. Within five years he took out a loan and started his own company. He treated all his men the way he wanted to be treated, and it worked. Within a few more years, business was booming.

But it didn't end there. Bubba took classes in architecture one night a week. His dream was to be able to build environmentally sound buildings that would be affordable to most people, buildings that would blend with the landscape, not neighborhood eyesores. It was still a while away, but it was something to reach for.

Why was Mel always a part of your life and you never really looked at her as a woman?

The question puzzled him. At first, when she'd confided in him, he hadn't been able to separate Mel his pal from Melanie the woman. But during the month they'd dated, something had changed. He'd made a conscious effort to *look* at her, to really see her.

What he saw he liked.

A long-legged, athletic blonde with enough stamina to keep up with him, a jock. She'd had to be, to keep up with her brothers. They'd teased her unmercifully, and Mel's only retaliation had been to excel. Tennis, swimming, baseball, basketball—she liked outdoor life, as much as he did.

It wasn't just physical, though. There were qualities in her he'd always taken for granted, never really thought about. The way she listened. It was a talent she had, making a person feel emotionally comfortable enough to open up and reveal himself. She had a sensitive outlook on life, too. Mel was a compassionate woman, and he liked that quality as well.

Her slight reserve covered a tremendous wellspring of passion. He'd been partially responsible for what she'd discovered about herself in his darkened bedroom their first night together, but she'd taken the lead over the weekend, no longer afraid. As comfortable as she was with her body, to come to terms with her sexuality had taken her a little more time.

She was everything he would ever want in a woman, so why the hesitation?

Don't rush things. Take it slow. You still don't know everything about her, even though you've been friends for so long. More than anything, she still needed his friendship right now. It was going to be rough, having a baby alone. If he'd thought it would help, he would have offered marriage, but Mel had the same stubborn streak of independence he possessed. She would look at him with that steady gaze of hers and never believe he'd fallen in love with her in eight weeks.

He didn't know himself. It was hard, switching gears: Mel the buddy to Melanie the woman. He had a responsibility to both of them not to push things, to let things evolve the way they were supposed to.

In the meantime, he would simply be there for her.

THE LATE SUMMER SUNSHINE was blinding as Melanie walked out of the complex of professional buildings in Santa Monica. She concentrated on merely putting one foot in front of the other. If she didn't, she'd start skipping, dancing along the sidewalk and grabbing the first person in her path. She was so eager to share her news with someone.

Pregnant. You're pregnant.

Exactly six weeks. She'd held her breath when she'd missed her first period, but as she'd never been one hundred percent regular, she hadn't been sure. Her breasts had been tender, but that could be water retention. She'd been tired, but she had been working hard.

Because it meant so very much to her, she didn't dare hope. Mel couldn't let herself believe it until her doctor smiled and told her the test they'd run was positive.

Her tentative due date was May 10. Her doctor had given her a prescription for vitamins and a diet sheet. Melanie was determined not to bloat out like a beached whale. She was going to do everything right. She knew this might be her only child, depending on how things went, and she wanted everything to be perfect.

Thank you, thank you, thank you. She chanted the words over and over, a silent prayer. The past year had been a mightmare. She'd never appreciated her health until something went wrong. Well, she was taking nothing for granted now.

It had been frightening, as if her body were no longer her own, taking control of her. Rebelling. She'd carried so much of the fear alone, not wanting to burden her family with her problems. Her father, in his sixties, had a heart condition. Her mother spent almost all her time looking after him. They didn't need to worry about anything else.

Her sisters would understand. Especially Sandy. The elder twin by two minutes, Sandy had always taken the time to listen, to try to understand another person's point of view. Stef would be a different matter. She was more temperamental than Sandy, quicker to voice what she thought without thinking of the consequences. She'd eventually come around, too.

Dick, the eldest of her brothers, lived on the East Coast with his wife and four children, and Mel didn't see him that often anyway. He'd been so far apart from her in age he was almost like a second father to her, not a brother. He'd lived at home for just a few years after she was born, so she didn't really know him that well.

And Donnie... *I will not let him spoil my day. I won't even think about his reaction.* Donnie thought it was his place to keep the family in line. His comments—what he thought about everyone—were voiced freely, whether you wanted to hear them or not. If you didn't, he'd get on the phone and call someone else in the family so he could have an audience. He reminded her of a crotchety old man trapped inside a younger body.

She stopped at the drugstore nearest her house and filled the prescription, then walked the rest of the way home. Letting herself into the house, she walked into her living room and sat down on her couch.

You're going to have a baby. She'd been surprised no one had questioned her sanity as she walked quickly along with the goofiest grin on her face. Lying back on the sofa, she patted her stomach.

She just couldn't stop smiling.

WHEN SHE OPENED HER EYES, Melanie realized she'd fallen asleep. Pushing her hair off her neck, she sat up on the couch and stared at the phone.

She wanted to call someone.

But who? Not Alicia. She didn't want to give her friend the news just yet. There would be too many questions involved. Sometimes she got the feeling Ali liked to live vicariously through others. She'd always wanted a child but just never found the right type of guy to settle down with—and Ali would never consider going it alone.

Mel just wasn't up to another lecture of how horrifyingly brave she was.

Her mother? No. No use worrying her until she was past the first trimester and the danger of a miscarriage lessened. Why give both her parents something else to be concerned about, until she was sure the baby was healthy?

Sandy? She ached to tell her oldest sister, but she was sure the news would reach her mother. Not Sandy. Stef was out of the question for now. Dick would probably need coaching to remember who she was.

She ran through each and every one of her friends and realized she had no one to share the news with.

Bubba. He'd be home shortly. She'd seen him at odd moments, when he left for work early in the morning and sometimes when he came home very late at night. She knew he was working hard, trying to keep things steady with his business. He'd be tired tonight, as he'd been for the past few weeks.

She hadn't seen that much of him since their weekend escapade with Joel. Was he ashamed to look at her after their shared intimacy? Did he want to let her down as gracefully as possible? Be a gentleman? She'd reassured him over the weekend that she didn't expect anything from him but that particular moment in time. Maybe he'd thought she wasn't telling the truth.

Impossible. You're letting your emotions run away with you. She searched for another plausible explanation. Maybe he was going out with someone. There was nothing to stop him. He hadn't mentioned anyone in a long time, but Bubba never really did. He'd never been one to boast of his exploits.

I expect to see a rainbow next time. The wind sock. Getting slowly to her feet, Mel padded down the hall and into the den on the west side of the house. Rummaging through one of the drawers, she pulled out the brightly striped wind sock and headed back out to her patio.

She and Bubba had thought up the idea of celebrating the holidays with various flags and banners. She'd bought this wind sock in Santa Barbara at a kite store. It was large, almost three feet long, and colored with every hue imaginable. Bubba had helped her set up a flagpole on one corner of her balcony, and she walked over to it now, taking down the banner that had been flying for the last couple of days. It had a blue background, with a fat, happy-faced yellow sun on it. To Mel, it was her end-of-the-summer salute.

She unfastened the banner, fastened the wind sock and hoisted it slowly up into the evening breeze. It was rapidly becoming dark. Bubba probably wouldn't see it until tomorrow morning. That was okay, because tomorrow was a Saturday and he didn't work on Saturday. Ever. Though he was a very hard worker, Bubba also believed in living for the moment, and his weekends were his own.

She gazed up at the wind sock as it caught the ocean breeze and began to snap briskly. Her hands strayed to her flat stomach and she rubbed it gently.

Here's to you, little one. I'm celebrating, even if no one else knows yet.

SATURDAY MORNINGS were always the same for Bubba—a brisk, five-mile run along the ocean. Normally he would have asked Mel along, but he was so full of tension from his workweek that he needed time alone. He ran until he was exhausted, stretched to his limit. It felt good. He liked to push himself, to try to go a little farther, a little faster.

Then into the hot tub. One of his knees gave him trouble at times, so he enjoyed the whirlpool effect of the hot water buffeting his legs. Henry followed him out onto the deck and plopped down in the shade of a begonia. He was burrowed underneath it so only his tail showed. Bubba knew his habits because Henry was nothing if not predictable. He liked to hide, wait for birds to appear on the back lawn, then race out and terrorize them.

Bubba paid him absolutely no attention as he rolled back the cover of the hot tub and climbed slowly inside. He pressed the rubber button on the side and the water began to bubble up from the bottom.

Heaven. He kept his eyes closed as his muscles began to relax. Resting his head on the edge of the tub, he let his mind wander. His patio was open, so the sun bathed his face and chest. In the distance he could hear the sound of an occasional car driving down the street, the laughter of children at play. Summer was coming to an end, and soon they'd all have to go back to school.

He'd hated school, being cooped up on days like this. It had been pure torture for the boy he'd been. Recess had helped, and later he made sure he staggered classes so he could sit in the sun for a few minutes at a time, to touch base again. He'd never understood either of his parents, his mother content hiding inside her house, his father behind a desk.

He wrinkled his forehead in concentration. What was that other noise? A snapping, whipping sound. He turned his face in the direction of the noise at the same time he opened his eyes.

The rainbow wind sock.

Mel.

He vaulted out of the hot tub, sending waves of water surging toward the begonia. Henry shot out from underneath it, but Bubba didn't even notice as he ran inside.

MELANIE WAS LYING on her couch, sick to her stomach. She'd tried to fry an egg that morning, but as soon as she saw it popping and sizzling in the frying pan, she'd turned off the gas and gone into the bathroom to throw up.

How had this suddenly happened to her? She'd been determined she wasn't going to have any morning sickness.

The knocking at her door sounded loud in her head.

"Just a minute." She got up, wondering who it could be this early in the morning. Dressed in underpants and a T-shirt, she walked over to the door and peered out the peephole.

Bubba.

"Mel? Answer the door!" He seemed impatient.

She opened it, using it to hide her lower half.

"Hi, Bubba." She knew she looked terrible, but she didn't even care.

"What's wrong?"

She shrugged. "Nerves, I guess. I was a little sick this morning."

"Can I come in?"

"In a second. Just let me get some clothes on." For some reason she was suddenly shy with him.

He waited out on the front steps until she went back up to her bedroom, pulled on an old pair of jeans, brushed and braided her hair and changed her T-shirt. Then she came back downstairs, determined to put on a more cheerful face.

"Come in."

He walked inside and they simply stared at each other for a minute.

Bubba made the first move. He simply reached out and pulled her into his arms, then wrapped her in a tight hug.

"Oh, Mel. Are you sure?"

She nodded her head.

"Then it happened over that weekend?"

She nodded again.

"Are you happy about it?"

"Yes." Then she burst into tears.

AMBIVALENCE. THAT'S WHAT IT IS. Bubba had decided the minute she started crying that a day at the beach would do both of them good. He helped her lock up the house, then bundled her inside his Honda and headed up Pacific Coast Highway, toward Zuma Beach.

She seemed to be relaxing. Anyway, he'd heard enough stories from his married friends of how women's temperaments changed during pregnancy. Mel had always been an emotional child; her feelings ran so strong he'd seen them literally make her sick.

Fresh air. I'm sure it'll be good for her. Get her out of the house, stop her from dwelling on things too much.

The beach was the perfect place. There was nothing like getting close to the water to put both of them in a better mood. He glanced over at her as he drove, then smiled. She was sleeping. Pregnancy would probably be harder on her body than a marathon.

Support. Give her support. He thought of Donnie, and his forehead wrinkled in concentration. He could be a bastard sometimes. If Donnie gave Mel too hard a time, he'd make it a point to fill her in on some of her brother's youthful escapades. Donnie was no saint—that was why his unrelenting, judgmental attitude was so hard to take. And annoying as hell. He hadn't been that way as a child. Or maybe he had, and it was just harder to take as they all got older. Sometimes Bubba wondered if they would have been friends at all if they hadn't first met in grade school. Donnie had not aged gracefully.

He wasn't selective about whom he criticized, and he didn't always restrict it to his family. He'd had many choice words to say about how Bubba conducted his life. The secret was to face him down, and Mel hadn't been able to do that yet. Pregnancy would only make her more vulnerable.

He let her sleep until they reached the beach, then he gently woke her, and they walked down to the shoreline without talking. He'd walked this beach a million times with Mel, but this time was different. It amazed him that they had actually succeeded. It was awe-inspiring. It was also frightening now that it was real.

And how much more frightening for her.

"Can we stop for a minute?" she asked.

"Sure." They walked up from the shoreline, to drier sand, and sat.

Melanie was concentrating on the waves, watching them as they crashed in and then hissed back out.

"You're the only person who knows, Bubba."

He didn't say anything, waiting for her to go on.

"I'm not going to tell anyone else until my fourth month."

"Okay." He took one of her hands in his. Her fingers were cool. She didn't squeeze back.

"I know what they'd all say if I told them now."

He knew, too, so he didn't say anything.

"That was the hardest part, coming home yesterday and not being able to tell anyone."

"You could have called me."

"I didn't want to bother you."

"Bother me, okay? You can't go through this completely alone."

"But I want you to know—I mean I don't want you to feel guilty or pressured or anything. Please, Bubba, this is so important to me. I don't want to do anything to wreck our friendship."

"You're not going to wreck anything."

"You'll tell me if I'm bothering you, okay?"

He smiled. If there was anyone in his life who was likely to bother him, it wasn't Mel.

"I'll let you know. Come on, let's head back. We have to celebrate properly. I'm taking you out to lunch."

He helped her up but was careful to pretend he didn't see the quick tears that ran down her cheeks before she brushed them away.

"What do you want to eat? Something that'll sit well in your stomach."

"Anything but eggs."

He laughed softly and put his arm around her shoulders as they started back toward the car.

Chapter Eight

Why didn't anyone tell me pregnancy could be so miserable? Mel thought as she leaned back against the toilet bowl, resting her head in her hands. She couldn't keep anything down. The smell of food cooking evoked an automatic response—straight to the bathroom. She was tired all the time, her breasts hurt, her head never failed to hit the pillow by nine in the evening. Even Alicia's tea-rose perfume made her gag.

Some mother you are. It was nothing like she'd thought it would be. Though she was still forcing herself to go to work each morning and putting on a cheery face for Alicia, it was hard. The worst part was feeling so totally alone. After Bubba took her to lunch to celebrate, she'd been scrupulously careful not to bother him. He saw the false-faced, smiling front as well.

There were some good moments, usually when her stomach was completely empty. It amazed Mel to realize that she'd never before seen so many pregnant women in her entire life. Maybe she'd simply never noticed them. Now she felt she had something in common with every pregnant women she saw. And babies—each time she saw one in its mother's arms, she wondered what her child would look like.

Some days she was crazily happy she'd been given this precious chance; others, she woke up and cried, staring at her ceiling, totally convinced she'd been insane ever to consider becoming a single mother.

One of her worst days had been when she'd read one of the small manuals her doctor had given her. It had described the trials of varicose veins and hemorrhoids: "But your husband will love you despite this, for the precious gift you are giving him." She'd put the pamphlet down and cried for a solid hour, convinced no man would ever want her again after she had given birth. Her body would be a gigantic mass of sags and stretch marks. Never mind that the doctor had given her the go-ahead on her regular exercise regime, she was convinced she was going to puff up like a soufflé.

The sound of the phone ringing brought her to attention. Thank God it was Saturday and she didn't have to go anywhere. Her plan for the day had been to force down some tea and crackers, then sit out in the October sunshine and knit, maybe finish the sweater she had started. Getting on her hands and knees, her stomach still tender, she crawled into the kitchen and reached up for the wall phone.

"Hello?"

"Mel? Bubba. I'm having some people over for a barbecue and I was wondering if you'd like to come by."

Anything would be better than staying in the house and feeling sorry for herself. It wasn't her normal nature to feel broody and self-centered. Perhaps this was just what she needed—a night out.

"Okay. Casual, right?" She almost laughed. *Nothing* at Bubba's house was anything but casual.

"Jeans and sweatshirts. You remember Terry and his girlfriend Laurie. It'll be just the four of us."

She remembered meeting the couple at Bubba's once before and liking them. This would be fun. "I'll be there, Bubba. What time, and do you want me to bring anything?"

"Seven and just yourself. How're you feeling these days, Mel?"

"Terrific." She was becoming an expert at lying through her teeth. "I'll see you then, Bubba."

After she hung up the phone, she lay down on the cool kitchen tile and closed her eyes.

As MELANIE ZIPPED UP her jeans, she studied herself critically in the mirror.

Thank God for small favors. At least my jeans still fit. In all the books on pregnancy she'd devoured in the past weeks, each had said a woman usually didn't start to show until the second trimester. She was only eight weeks pregnant, so she still fit her clothes.

Some of them, anyway. She'd deliberately picked a baggy sweatshirt to hide her large breasts. They made her self-conscious, the way they stuck out in front of her. She still looked good, though. The sweatshirt was a pale peach color, the palm trees silk-screened on the front. She looked very casual.

She'd washed her hair and pulled it up on top of her head in a casual topknot; she'd even applied a little makeup. She'd considered doing her nails, but the minute she opened the polish bottle she felt the familiar tightening of her stomach, so she recapped it quickly.

Now if you just stay downwind of the barbecue. But evenings were usually better than mornings. She might even be able to eat.

Glancing at her bedside clock, she saw it read seven-twelve. Picking up her bag, she walked quickly out of the room before she had a chance to change her mind and remain hidden in her bedroom.

"ANYONE FOR THE HOT TUB afterward?" Bubba asked, expertly flipping a hamburger on the grill.

Melanie tried to smile. The smells were getting to her, but so far no one had noticed how she'd edged closer and closer to Bubba's back door.

"Sounds good." Laurie, a petite brunette with short, curly hair and a quick smile, was dishing potato salad onto her paper plate.

"I'll go for it." Terry, lying in the hammock to the side of the large patio, was waiting for the ribs.

"Mel?" Bubba directed his gaze to hers.

"Fantastic!" *Boy, you're getting good at this.* She wanted nothing more than to go home and lie down.

"I think you left a suit here from last time, Mel. I put it in the back bathroom."

"Maybe I'll go change now." She grasped the chance eagerly.

She was just in time. With quiet efficiency, she threw up, then sat down on the bathroom floor and took deep breaths.

You'll feel better now that your stomach is empty. One of the worst things about getting sick was that she had to face food again. She couldn't just keep not eating; it wasn't good for the baby.

The black suit was draped over a towel hanging on the shower door. Mel pulled it down and studied it. It was a slinky maillot, with high-cut French legs and a low-cut front. Quickly unsnapping her jeans, she wriggled into the bottom half.

So far so good.

The top was a disaster. The low-cut bodice barely covered her swelling breasts. There was something obscene about them, the way they looked ready to explode at any second.

Ugly. You look ugly. She could feel quick tears gathering in her eyes. More than anything, just for this one night she didn't want to be pregnant.

"Mel?" It was Bubba, knocking softly at the door.

She swallowed the tightness in her throat. "I'm okay."

There was a pause; then he said, "You don't sound so good. What's wrong?"

She took a deep breath. "It doesn't fit."

"Let me see." He started in the bathroom door, and she turned away from him, embarrassed.

"Mel, what's wrong with it? You look great."

Sure—from the back. Slowly, her hands over her breasts, she turned and faced him.

He studied her for a moment, and she was so glad there was nothing in his eyes but quiet kindness. If he'd made any kind of joke or told her she looked great from a guy's point of view, she would have burst into tears.

"Why don't I get you one of my T-shirts? You can just wear it over the top of the suit."

"Why don't I just sit in the hammock and watch the three of you?"

He put his arm around her, gently massaging her tense shoulder. "It'll relax you. It's okay, I turned the heat down this morning, so it shouldn't be too hot."

Without another word he left, returning within a minute with a black T-shirt.

"Come on, put this on."

She lifted up her arms and he slid the shirt over her. It was perfect. While she didn't look like something on the cover of *Sports Illustrated*, at least she was comfortable.

She rolled up the sleeves, then took the slack at the bottom and tied it in a knot at the side. "Thanks, Bubba."

"Hey, you look great. You design sweaters—they'll think it's the latest fashion. Do you feel better?"

She nodded her head. He took her hand and they walked back out to the patio.

It turned out to be a fun evening. Mel picked at a chicken breast and concentrated on the fresh fruit salad. Later in the evening, she leaned back in the hot tub and felt her body begin to unwind.

"I love that T-shirt, the way you tied it. That's a big look this fall, isn't it? The kind of oversize look, I mean." Laurie's dark eyes sparkled, her hair curled damply around her face.

Oversize is right. "Yes, it is." She almost jumped as she felt Bubba give the part of her arm that was underneath the water a quick squeeze. "All the sweaters I knit for fall and winter were unstructured. They're just so easy to pull on."

When there was a lull in her conversation with Laurie, she glanced over at Bubba. He was smiling and she smiled back—genuinely this time.

She enjoyed herself. Laurie and Terry were fun to talk to. By the end of the evening, Laurie had promised to stop by her shop, and all four of them had agreed they had to take in a movie or spend a day at the beach, just to get together again and talk.

She helped Bubba clean up, being careful not to concentrate on the food. When the last bowl was in the refrigerator and the patio was completely cleaned up, she went back into the bathroom and changed into her jeans and sweatshirt.

He was in the living room lighting a fire when she walked in.

"I had a terrific time. They're really nice. Thanks for thinking of me."

"I'm glad." He sat down on the couch and patted the space beside him. "Sit down with me for a little bit and catch me up on things."

She wasn't quite sure what he meant and was surprised when he began to ask her about her doctor's visits, how she was feeling, what she was eating and if she was taking vitamins. After an initial hesitation, she felt it all come spilling out of her. *This* is what she'd wanted—someone to share all of it with.

When there was a lull in the conversation, she yawned, trying to smother the yawn with her hand so he wouldn't notice.

"I'm tiring you out," he said softly. "Lie down on the end of the couch while I fix the fire, then I'll walk you home."

When he finished, he stood up and turned toward her, but she was already fast asleep.

As SHE STARTED to drift awake, she smiled. It was so warm and cozy, so peaceful. Something was snapping in the background, and she wasn't sure what it was. She must have fallen asleep on her sofa again; she recognized the feel of the afghan on top of her, the pillow underneath her head.

But when she slowly opened her eyes, she realized that she wasn't home. Bubba was sitting on the far end of the long couch. The afghan covering her was the one she'd crocheted him for his last birthday; the pillow was from his bedroom. It even had his scent on it.

He was studying her. Something flickered in his eyes so quickly she wasn't sure if it was a reflection from the fire or just her imagination. Then he smiled at her, reached down and squeezed her foot through the afghan.

"You went out like a light, so I let you sleep."

Her hair had come undone from its casual topknot, so as she sat up she pulled out the rest of the pins and let it cascade around her shoulders. Pushing the heavy mass back with her fingers, she stretched slightly.

"I should be heading back."

"No hurry. If you want to, you can crash on the couch. It's Sunday tomorrow; you can sleep in. It won't bother me at all."

It was appealing, the thought of not moving when she felt so good. "You don't have to twist my arm," she said, snuggling beneath the afghan.

He stared at her for a moment longer, then said quietly, "I'll lock up, then."

She lay against the pillow, listening to the sounds he made as he locked the sliding door and then pulled the drapes shut. Lights were clicked off until the only illumination was from the fire.

He came back and tossed another T-shirt near her feet. "I thought it might be a little uncomfortable, sleeping in your clothes."

"Thanks." She waited until he headed upstairs and the house was silent to pull her sweatshirt over her head, unhook her bra and pull on the T-shirt. It smelled of Bubba, too, of the clean scent of the laundry soap she knew he used. Sliding her jeans off, she dropped her clothes onto the floor and curled up under the afghan.

Within minutes, she was alseep again.

WHEN SHE WOKE UP to a darkened living room, it took her a minute to figure out why. Then she heard the slight noise in the kitchen—the refrigerator door shutting, the sound of liquid being poured.

She sat up on the couch, glancing in the direction of the noise. Bubba came back out of the kitchen, dressed in a pair of running shorts, a glass in his hand.

"Bubba?"

He stopped. "Damn, Mel, I'm sorry. I didn't mean to wake you."

"What's wrong?"

He smiled. "The barbecue sauce was a little too spicy for me; I got thirsty."

"Oh."

"Do you want something to drink?"

"I'd love it. I'll—" She stopped in midsentence, realizing she had nothing on but a T-shirt and her panties. She couldn't just hop off the couch and parade in front of him.

"Stay there. I'll get you something. Orange juice okay?"

"Fine."

When he came back out of the kitchen, he sat down on the end of the couch, and they drank in silence. The fire was reduced to glowing embers, but the living room still felt warm.

She set her glass down on the coffee table and sighed. "Thanks. That was great."

"No problem."

She realized he was about to leave, so she spoke quickly. "Bubba, I wanted to thank you for letting me ramble on about everything. It felt so good, sharing it all with you. It's so hard, sometimes, to keep it all bottled up inside."

"You can tell me anything, Mel."

"Oh, Bubba." She leaned forward in a purely spontaneous gesture, wound her arms around his neck and kissed him.

She felt his body tense for a fraction of a second, then his arms came up around her, holding her close.

With a quickness that astonished her, the kiss deepened, changed from friendly to totally erotic. Not thinking, not *wanting* to think, she answered him, parting her lips and offering him anything he wanted to take from her.

He broke the kiss as abruptly as the mood had shifted, picked up the glasses and strode quickly into the kitchen. Mel sat in the dark, her fingers lightly touching her lips. That one kiss brought back all her memories of the few nights she'd spent with him. She'd pushed those thoughts to the back of her mind, partially because they scared her and partially because she didn't want to lose the friendship she had with him.

A larger part yearned to touch him again, to experience the feelings she'd only felt with him. If she was totally honest with herself, she wanted to be close to him, to share, to be held in his arms, to hold him, to comfort and be comforted. To love him.

She felt his presence before he stopped by the sofa.

"I'm sorry, Mel. I didn't have anything like that in mind when I asked you if you wanted to sleep on the couch. I want you to believe that."

"I do," she whispered.

"Good ni—" He stopped talking as she linked her fingers with his, then stood up, letting the afghan fall away from her.

"I do believe you," she said softly, standing against him, then sliding her arms up around his neck. "But I don't want you to go upstairs."

"Mel, I—"

"Don't talk, Bubba. Please don't talk."

Then what she'd felt in his kiss slowly became reality. His large hands slid slowly over her back and her hips, then cupped her buttocks and pulled her against him as he lowered his mouth to hers.

Everything she'd ever wanted was in that kiss, bringing her blood to life, making her tremble in anticipation. She didn't want him to go slowly, didn't want them both to wait for what was ahead. There was so much left to explore with this man, a lifetime's worth of sensual, loving feelings.

Her legs were shaking as he lowered her to the couch. Within seconds she was lying on top of him, between his legs, as he cradled her face with his hands and continued to kiss her. A hard knot of tension began to build inside her, demanding to be set free. Wanting to journey quickly to that point, she answered his kisses with her own, letting him know by her slight aggression that she was impatient for him, hungry for the feel of his naked body next to hers.

As if he were able to guess what was inside her head, he reached for the hem of her T-shirt and pulled it up, easing his hands underneath, holding her sides. Just the tips of his long fingers brushed the sides of her breasts, and she groaned against his mouth, wanting more. Needing more. How had he reduced her to a quivering mass of need within minutes of his first kiss?

It was the same for him. She knew it on an entirely instinctive, feminine level. She knew it by the way his muscled body shuddered slightly when she ran her fingers down his chest, touched the flat, male nipples. His arms were tense with suppressed energy, holding everything in check for her.

"Touch me," she whispered, breaking the kiss to tell him what she wanted, surprised at the words that seemed to spring out of her mouth with a will of their own. In answer, he slowly stripped the shirt off her. When he tossed it to the floor, he grasped her buttocks and pulled her slowly, pleasurably, up the length of his body until he could reach the tip of her breast with his lips.

He suckled gently at first, as if afraid of hurting her. She moaned, low in her throat, as he kissed first one, then the other. There was nothing for her but his touch, the feel of his lips, the warmth of his hard, muscled body beneath hers. Heat seemed to radiate up from him, rushing through her body with shimmering waves. They were lifting her, pressing her closer against him.

She felt his hands move down her back, underneath the elastic band, skinning off the last barrier. She welcomed it, answering him by easing her fingers down the front of his shorts and cupping part of the hard, hot proof of his masculinity in her hand. He made an anguished sound in the back of his throat when she touched him, his head went back and he gasped as if he'd run a long distance. Swiftly she peeled away the last piece of clothing and lay down on top of him once again.

He shifted to his side, bringing her along with him. Still, he held her body against his as if by doing so he could meld their skins together, submerge them into each other. He continued to kiss her as his hands explored her slowly, drawing out the exquisite agony of anticipation. She didn't protest when he eased her leg up over his, when his fingers stroked her inner thighs and moved upward.

She reached for him, wanting him to move inside her, touch her as deeply as possible. But he stilled her hand, took it and placed it around his neck.

"Wait. Just a little more."

He touched her again, gently opening her, moving directly to her center and starting a deep, inner pulsing, a burning ache. She buried her face against his neck as her legs started to tremble. She could hear his deep breathing, feel the steady, rapid beating of his heart. It seemed to merge with hers, drumming her blood wildly throughout her body until she thought she would burn right out of her skin.

He slowly eased her beneath him, sliding her legs wide apart, touching her the entire time. He kissed her flushed face, then caught her lips with his, covering her mouth with his own at the same moment his body moved. A slow silken movement, it brought him right to the heart of her. He entered her slowly, carefully, all the more sensuous for controlling his power.

She broke the kiss, a sob escaping her as she climaxed powerfully, just his touch enough to set her on fire. The feel of his heat and strength, the deepness of his thrust, everything melded in a white-hot burst of sensation that caused her hips to jerk up tautly against his, caused her to cry out his name as he lay perfectly still, imbedded inside her.

He waited until she could bear sensation again, then began to move: slow, deep, pleasurable thrusts. This time she concentrated on him, wanting him to receive as much pleasure as she had had, but he caught her up in the heat of his possession, so much so that when she peaked again her fingers clenched the hard muscles in his shoulders, as if trying to climb inside his body and be one with him forever.

As their breathing slowed and their heartbeats stopped racing, there was no need to pull up the afghan. Melanie had never felt so warm, so flushed with pleasure, as she curled up against his hard body. There wasn't any softness about Bubba. He was all masculine muscle and strength. She snuggled closer as his arm came around her shoulders, pillowed her cheek against his hair-roughened chest.

Neither of them spoke. What had happened had robbed them of words. She closed her eyes, feeling his hand gently stroking her back, knowing that she wanted to wake up and have that same hand touching her, his arm securely around her. Holding her close to him, against his heart.

IT COULD HAVE BEEN minutes or hours, Bubba wasn't sure which, before his eyes fluttered open. The living room was dark; the fire had died to a few glowing embers.

His arm was falling asleep. *Now that's romantic,* he thought as he eased his arm out from underneath Mel's cheek. She didn't wake up as he slowly got up off the couch and went upstairs. Grabbing two pillows and several blankets, he went back downstairs and put them by the fire. Walking to the couch, he studied Mel, curled up underneath the afghan he'd tucked around her.

You can't go on this way any longer. He knew what he felt. The hard thing would be convincing Mel. He was scared to talk to her about his new, deep feelings for her, because he was convinced she would push him away. Even as a child, Mel had never wanted pity. She'd been independent and tough, the result of being the youngest in the family.

But it's not pity you're offering her. They had to talk about this sooner or later. It might as well be right now. He sat back down on the large couch and eased himself underneath the afghan, curling his body around hers. He liked to watch her sleep, and he did that. He positioned his body so their heads were close together.

Then he reached out a hand and stroked her cheek gently with one finger. First, her nose crinkled and she moved her face away. Then, as he continued his light caress, Mel moaned softly and tried to bury her face in the pillow. Bubba leaned over and kissed the back of her neck.

"Hey, Mel," he whispered.

"Mmm," she responded.

He smiled. She was a morning person, not given to waking up at all hours of the night. But this was special.

"Mel?"

Her eyes slowly fluttered open, a dazed expression in them before they slowly cleared. He could almost see the workings of her mind as she began to realize where she was.

"Oh, Bubba," she began, and he put his finger over her mouth. If there was one thing he didn't want from Mel, it was an apology.

He moved his head so his mouth was close to her ear, so he wasn't looking at her face. So she had a little privacy, could take the time to feel through what he was going to say.

In the end, when he said the words, he felt as if all the tightness was leaving his chest. It had taken so much effort, laughing and joking when all he'd wanted to do was tell her how much she meant to him.

"Mel, I love you." His voice was barely a whisper, but he was sure she heard it.

He could feel the slight stiffening of her body, the way she was pulling away from him, so he wrapped his arms around her body and pressed her against the warmth of his.

"I've loved you for a long time. I don't know when it started or how, I just know I love you." He stroked her back slowly, wanting to ease the tension and fear out of her body, wanting to make her feel safe enough to reciprocate, because he knew she loved him. Mel wasn't the type of woman to put that much feeling behind lovemaking if there wasn't an emotional involvement. She couldn't fake emotion.

"Every time I've wanted to talk to you about the way I feel, you've pushed me away. But I just want you to know—" he took a deep breath "—I love you and I don't think it's the kind of love that will go away in a few weeks. Do you know what I mean?"

He felt her slowly nod her head.

"And it's not just the baby."

He heard her take a deep, shuddering breath.

"I don't expect an answer right now," he continued slowly. His chest was slowly starting to tighten again. In his fantasies, she would have answered, "But I've always loved you, too!" But he knew Mel, knew how stubborn she could be. It wasn't meant to happen that way. Not yet.

"I don't want you to feel pressured. I just want you to know how I feel." He kissed the soft skin underneath her ear. "I love you, Mel, and it's not going to go away. Not ever."

When she didn't answer, he levered himself up on his elbow and looked down at her face. She was perfectly still, but tears welled in her eyes and one slowly spilled over and ran down her cheek.

"Hey." He kissed her face, reached with one finger and caught the tear. "Hey." The other one spilled over and he kissed its path. "Mel, it's all right. I *love* you. I can't think of any other way to say it. I'm not very good with words."

"Oh, Bubba," she whispered. There was a touch of sadness in her voice. "I never meant for this to happen. You believe me, don't you?"

"I know, Mel, but it did. It's like one of those waves that pulls you under. You fight it for a little bit, then you just let it take you and it feels good, you know?"

She nodded.

"I don't want to fight it anymore, Mel. I don't want to be with you and pretend you don't matter to me." He took a deep breath. "So no matter what you may think or what you want out of all of this, I just want you to know how I feel about you. Okay?"

She nodded, looking so miserable it tore at his heart. So he gathered her up in his arms and held her tightly.

"Go back to sleep," he whispered. "I'm going to be here in the morning." He held her as her breathing slowly deepened; then he carefully got up and made a more comfortable bed out of pillows and blankets by the fire. He picked her up and lowered her into the makeshift bed, then tucked the covers around her.

Sliding in beside her, he put his arm around her and she turned, nuzzling her cheek against his shoulder. He kissed her forehead.

"I mean it, Mel," he said softly. As he lay in the darkness, he formulated his plan, and as the first faint streaks of sunlight began to slip across the blankets he smiled and slowly closed his eyes.

WHEN SHE WOKE UP, she was surprised to find them on the floor in front of the fire, in the midst of a nest of pillows and blankets. Bubba was sleeping soundly, the faintest of smiles on his face.

For a moment, embarrassment took over, and she thought of pulling on her clothes and sneaking back to her house. But looking at his face, she couldn't. What had happened last night was so very special. More than lovemaking, there had been something there she didn't want to think about.

As Bubba's feelings for her were deepening, so were her own for him. Somehow, somewhere along the line, he'd stopped being simply Bubba her friend. A new dimension had been slowly added on. She knew exactly what he'd been feeling last night because she felt the same.

Her feelings toward him were expanding, circles of emotion that were growing wider and wider, letting her view him in an entirely different way.

I love him. She lay back down in the pillows, watched his chest rise and fall and studied his face: the familiar blond hair, lightened by the sun, the laugh lines at the corner of his eyes. He hadn't shaved that weekend, and there was a slightly darker stubble along his jawline. She wanted to trace his chin, wanted to touch him. But she couldn't wake him up when he looked so tired.

So she simply watched him, and as she did her hand slid down to her stomach and she wondered at how lucky she was. If she couldn't burden Bubba with an instant family, at least she still had his child and could someday tell her she had been created out of total, pure love.

Chapter Nine

Melanie woke with a start later in the morning. It was as predictable as clockwork. Glancing quickly at Bubba, she was glad to see he was still asleep. The last thing she wanted was for him ever to see her in this condition.

Getting up as carefully and swiftly as she could, disregarding her clothing, she ran toward the bathroom.

BUBBA ROLLED OVER, reaching for Mel. He was half awake and remembering how they'd spent most of the night. It was exactly the way he wanted to spend the morning.

When he couldn't find her amid the tangle of pillows and blankets he'd carried down last night, he opened his eyes.

She left. Then he heard the faint noise, like coughing. Leaping to his feet, he headed in the direction of the sound.

He stopped outside the bathroom door. Mel was sick. He didn't think about the fact that he was stark naked as he opened the bathroom door.

She was kneeling by the toilet, her body quivering with the force of her distress. The fragile line of her bare back moved him; she looked so helpless and vulnerable as she knelt on the bathroom floor. Quickly, with a minimum of movement, he reached for her head, held her, steadied her. He smoothed back her hair and caught it in his fist.

She made a feeble attempt to push him away, but the next wave of sickness overwhelmed her and she couldn't move. He felt her give in, sensed when her body simply accepted the support he offered.

Afterward, she looked so ashamed by the whole thing his heart went out to her.

"Come on, Mel, lie down. I'll get you some 7-Up."

She looked as if she was about to cry. He couldn't stand to see her this way, so he picked her up and carried her upstairs to his bed. Tucking her in, he raced down to the kitchen and was back within minutes, glass in hand.

"Drink this."

She did, tiny sips, barely a third of the glass. Then she set it down on the nightstand and slid deeper underneath the covers, her face pale and exhausted-looking.

"Have you called your doctor about this?" Bubba asked.

She shook her head. She looked terrible; her face was too pale, and tired lines were etched beneath her eyes.

"Give me her number."

"No." She looked at him for a second, then closed her eyes again, her expression totally defeated. "I'll call Monday morning."

"Mel, I've heard about morning sickness, but this doesn't look good to me."

She held out her hand and he took it, squeezing it gently. Then, not knowing what else to do, he lay down beside her, outside the covers, and enfolded her in his arms. It was several minutes before he realized she was silently crying.

"Mel? Honey, tell me what's wrong."

The whispered words were hard to decipher among her quiet sobs, but he finally made out what she was trying to say.

"I'm a failure, Bubba. I can't do this right. I've been so sick, even from the beginning. I kept trying to pretend everything was all right. I thought maybe if I pretended hard enough, it would all go away." She took a deep breath.

He wiped the tears away from her eyes but didn't say anything.

"I hate the whole thing! My breasts hurt. I'm crabby. Bubba, I'm not like this, I'm *not*, but I'm so tired of throwing up and aching all over."

Her words froze him, chilling his entire body. "Mel, did I...did I hurt you last night when we—"

"No." She began to cry harder, and he kissed her cheek and slid up the bed so she was resting her head against his shoulder. "That was the only time I felt good. I don't understand how something so wonderful could make me feel so awful."

His heart was breaking for her. "Mel, I'm calling your doctor now."

And he did. He kept calling until he got through, listened to what the doctor had to say, and hung up the phone. The entire time he'd stroked Mel's forehead lightly, wishing he could give her even one-tenth of his strength.

And feeling so helpless.

"I'm going to make you some toast, then we're going to take a drive."

"Where?" She didn't sound enthusiastic.

"We're going to see your doctor, Mel. She agreed to come to her office and see you. Something isn't right here."

He stayed with her the entire day, took her to her doctor's office, listened to her advice, then drove home. When he pulled the car into the driveway, he cut the engine and looked over at Mel.

"I think you should take it," he said quietly, referring to the medication her doctor had prescribed for her.

"No. I keep thinking—I couldn't stand it if something went wrong because I had to take a pill."

"Honey, you heard what she said, that every woman is different. She wouldn't prescribe anything that would hurt you. She told you some of her other patients used it."

"Bubba, you've been wonderful and I appreciate what you did for me, but I'd like to go home now."

He knew her too well. She was on the edge of breaking down again and didn't want him to see.

Sometimes Mel tried too hard to protect other people's feelings.

"I want you to come home with me."

He hadn't been sure what her reaction was going to be, but it wasn't what he expected. She turned quickly in her seat and unlocked the door with shaking fingers. Stumbling outside, she began to walk quickly toward her front door, the white bag from the pharmacy clutched tightly in one of her hands.

"Mel!" He leapt out of the car and raced after her. Catching her at the door, he grabbed both her arms, careful all the while not to hurt her.

"Mel, let me help you. Please."

She started to cry then, and he took the key out of her purse and unlocked the door. He settled her on the couch, and sat down next to her as he pulled her into his arms. Then he rocked her, crooning unintelligible sounds, trying to soothe her.

When she stopped, he went into the bathroom and came back with a box of tissues. She blew her nose and looked down at the carpet in front of the sofa.

"Mel, I'm the only person who can help you. I'm the only one who knows."

She shook her head silently. Her voice was clogged and nasal. "I didn't want this to happen, you feeling guilty and having to—"

"Is that really why you think I'm here with you?"

She met his gaze and he almost smiled. There was something independent and defiant in her gaze, even though her face was splotchy and her eyes red-rimmed.

"Yes."

"Mel." He picked up her hand and studied it. "I thought we were closer than that. You know me. I don't let guilt run my life. I'm with you because I want to be with you."

"Do you mean that?" Her voice shook, and he put his arms around her shoulders, giving her a brief hug.

"Absolutely. Now go upstairs and lie down. I'm going to fix you something to eat and then we're both going to take a nap."

She opened her mouth to say something but seemed to reconsider. He narrowed his eyes mockingly and said, "There's no way you're going to get out of this one."

"I...okay."

HE MOVED INTO HER HOUSE that same week, simply wanting to protect her, help her. He slept in her bed but never touched her. Henry, not liking being confined to an empty house, moved in, too. It wasn't all bad. There were fun times living with Mel. It was rare she got to the point she had that Sunday, and he chalked it up to the fact that before she'd been holding in so many fears and feelings of inadequacy. He wondered about her family. As close as they had seemed to him, she still hadn't told any of them.

Their life together fell into a pleasant rhythm. They shopped together. He cooked. They split their evenings between their two houses. When she felt good, Mel would knit, and he was amazed that she could turn out a sweater in eighteen hours. He showed her the plans of several houses he'd started to design and was flattered in the interest she took. She made several very practical suggestions, as well.

When she felt better, her goofy sense of humor returned. Those were the times he enjoyed the most because he knew she wasn't hurting.

One night, after he came home from work, he picked her up and they drove to the local supermarket. It was the week before Thanksgiving, and Mel was planning on going home to her parents. Knowing Bubba would be spending the holiday alone—his mother was visiting her sister on the East Coast; his father had simply stopped seeing that much of his son after the separation—she'd asked him to come home with her.

They entered the market with Mel checking and rechecking her list. Bubba grabbed a cart, discarded it because it had a bad wheel, then grabbed another. They started down the first aisle.

"Where to first?" He was surprised to find he liked doing little things like this with Mel. There was a strong streak of protectiveness he felt toward her, and it had nothing to do with the fact that she was pregnant with his child. She was such a paradox to him— so strong emotionally, so fragile in other ways. Her moods never ceased to amaze him, but with the help of one of the doctor's pamphlets, he knew they would pass soon.

"Cranberries. We're responsible for the relish." She was dressed in a pair of corduroy pants and an oversize sweater. Her hair was pulled up off her face in a braid that hung straight down her back like a golden skein.

They were halfway down one aisle when she stopped. Bubba was used to this by now. He knew the reality of her pregnancy was beginning to hit home. He studied her body as she slept, knew her tummy was beginning to swell. You wouldn't notice it if you weren't looking for it—but he was.

"Mel? Cranberries?" He crooked his finger at her. "C'mere, you."

She did, looking as if she were coming out of a slight daze. Then she surprised him, walking straight into his arms, giving him a hug and a kiss and climbing into the metal cart.

"I sense a little babying is in order," he teased, tugging at her braid as he started to wheel the shopping cart. An older man, studying the labels of various soup cans, turned and stared as Bubba continued to push Mel down the aisle.

She simply reached up and placed her hand over Bubba's.

THANKSGIVING WAS nerve-racking. The good news was that Donnie couldn't make dinner, the bad was that Sandy's instincts were working overtime, and Bubba suspected she knew something was up.

Mel was a quiet, high-strung nervous wreck. Dinner wasn't pleasant, and Bubba made excuses to leave as soon as they could. Driving back up the 405 North to Santa Monica, they talked.

"How come things were so different when we were kids?" he asked. "Or were my perceptions completely wrong in the first place?"

"I think you liked being with us because it was noisy and things were always going on." She sighed. "My parents are getting older, Bubba. I see it every time I visit them."

"Yeah."

"Daddy looks so tired. After his first heart attack, I don't know, he never seemed the same after that."

"I remember." Mel had been sixteen. He still remembered seeing her white face at the hospital. He'd come back home to help her family as soon as he'd heard.

"And Mother—she tries so hard to keep everyone together and not fighting. But as all of us got older, I think we just grew different ways."

"You can grow in different ways and still not lose touch. Relationships change, Mel. Sometimes even for the better."

"I suppose so. Did you get enough to eat?"

He sensed she was deliberately changing the subject, not wanting to skirt that issue again. She was determined to keep him at bay.

She thinks it's because she's pregnant. He tightened his hand on the steering wheel, frustration making him tense. *I'll just have to use Henry's technique— hang around long enough and she won't be able to get rid of me.*

It was small consolation, but it would get him through the next few months.

MEL'S SECOND TRIMESTER changed the way she felt about being pregnant. One morning she woke up and realized her morning sickness had stopped. She felt better, had more energy and wasn't as moody. Her body seemed to be her own again, but on the other hand, her pregnancy started to show.

Bubba refused to go back home, even though she wasn't sick anymore. He liked to lie in bed with her and explore the new roundness to her tummy. He made her laugh by putting his mouth near her navel and talking to the baby. And he made up a string of ridiculous names.

She knew she should have put a stop to it, made Bubba realize that he didn't have to hang around all the time, but she honestly couldn't. She enjoyed his company, especially at this time.

"Skip," he said one morning. They were out on her deck, having a late brunch on a Sunday afternoon. "Skip is a good name for a prospective surfing champion."

"That's a nickname, not a name," she said calmly, deliberately not looking up from the Calendar section of the *Los Angeles Times*. If she met his eyes, she would dissolve into laughter.

"Nicknames are important," Bubba continued. "That baby book said that nicknames are a symbol of status. Look at me; I was Bubba all through high school and college."

She deliberately arched an eyebrow at him. "Exactly. Look at you. I could call you Robert if you'd like."

"It makes me feel like I'm three hundred years old."

"Bubba, you'll never get old."

Mel found she treasured her time with Bubba. She loved laughing and talking with him; she needed his steady support. Her body was changing as rapidly as her emotions. Before, the idea of their baby had been an abstract concept and pregnancy a state of sickness; now the baby was a reality to her, frightening in a different way. That same morning, before she'd stepped into the shower, she'd studied her body carefully in the full-length mirror.

There's no turning back now. She didn't want to turn back, but it was new, uncharted emotional territory all the same.

When she thought back to what she'd put Bubba through during the first three months of her pregnancy, she couldn't believe he still wanted to see her face, let alone spend massive amounts of time with her. They didn't sleep together, simply slept with each other. She woke up many mornings to find him watching her, his hand gently resting on her abdomen.

"How did you ever put up with me?" she asked, pouring him another cup of coffee.

"It was nothing. All in a day's work." He gave her a mock-smug look.

"Come on, Bubba! It couldn't have been fun for you."

"No, it was in a way. It was strange seeing you veer all over the place and cry all the time, but there are things I remember that were funny."

"Refresh my memory," she said dryly.

He took a sip of his coffee. "Remember the night I woke up and you weren't in bed but I found you crawling to the bathroom along the hall rug?"

She could feel herself starting to blush. "I never—"

"Do you remember what you said to me when I asked you what you were doing down there?"

"I don't have the total recall you seem to have. No, I don't remember."

He was smiling broadly now. "You said, 'I have to stay low to the ground because if I die I don't want to fall down.'"

"Did I really say that?"

"I swear that's what I heard."

"I don't know, those weeks just kind of all strung together. It was one big daze to me."

"You were so funny, Mel, when you weren't crying."

"I really did cry a lot—I remember that."

They ate the rest of their breakfast in a comfortable silence. Mel had made blueberry muffins, and Bubba had whipped up cheese-and-avocado omelets. It was sunny for the middle of December, but a breeze was blowing, so they were both dressed warmly.

"Still up for the beach?" Bubba asked as he drained his third and last cup of coffee.

"You couldn't keep me away at this time of year."

"I'm going to go over and feed the great white whale, then I'll come back and pick you up. Deal?"

"You're on."

After Bubba left, using the path he'd worn by vaulting over the fence that separated their backyards, Mel cleared off the small picnic table and went upstairs to her bedroom.

She packed her beach bag with a towel, sunscreen and the Sunday crossword puzzle, then she began to walk down the stairs. The doorbell sounded and she smiled.

So like Bubba, to be impatient to get to the beach.

"Just a second," she yelled as she ran quickly to her refrigerator and pulled out two cans of apple juice. Stuffing them into her tote, she took a last glance in the hallway mirror. Faded jeans and running shoes. An intricately patterned Aran sweater. Her hair was pulled back into a ponytail, and she didn't need makeup. She felt good, and it showed.

The bell pealed again and she laughed. "Hold on!" Running to the door, she yanked it open, then felt her stomach clench in complete shock.

Donnie. Oh, my God.

"Mel, I was in town so I decided—"

She froze as his gaze took in her thickened waistline, her protruding stomach. Slowly, ever so slowly, he surveyed every inch of her body; then his eyes locked with hers. They were the same deep blue, but they were glittering in a way she'd seen before and didn't like.

"So when did you get marrried?" he asked quietly. "No one told me anything about an addition to the family. Who's the lucky man?" His tone was just the tiniest bit insulting, and she suspected he'd summed up the situation for himself.

"Donnie…" Her stomach felt as if it were being shredded to bits, but she kept her eyes level with his, refusing to plead or look away.

"Who is he?"

"Donald..." She knew he hated to be called Donald. "Donald, I didn't get married." There. It was out.

"Oh, this is just great!" Without asking whether he could come in or not, Donnie stormed past her. Mel slammed the door after him and followed him into her living room.

"Is this what you meant when you said it was time you lived alone? What have you been doing in this house, Mel? Huh? Are you crazy?"

"Donnie, I had to—"

"Had to *what*? Go after anything in pants? Why didn't you call *me* if the bastard didn't want to marry you! Can't you do anything right?"

"Donnie, *that's enough*!"

"No, *this is enough*!" He whirled on her, disgust etched into every facial feature. "Damn it, Mel, I thought you were a responsible adult, but it's clear to me now you're still a child. Do Mom and Dad know about this?"

"No. They don't. I was going to tell them when—"

"You were going to tell them *when*? Christmas Eve? What a nice little surprise! Well, don't be too upset if they aren't exactly ecstatic with joy!"

"Goddamn it, Donnie, will you listen to me—"

"No. You listen to me and you listen good. You've got a week to get out of this house and go home where you belong. Mom can send you to Aunt Katherine, and you can remain there—"

"This is *not* the eighteenth century!"

"You can stay there until you have the little bastard, then we can make arrangements."

A cold, numbing anger was slowly filling her body, making her shake with pure rage. "You can't walk in here and take over as if I were some kind of— Get out! Get out right now before I throw you out!"

For a minute he seemed to back off, then he turned on his heel and marched to her door, flinging it open.

"Mel, don't even think for one minute I'm going to let you continue this way! Since Dad had his heart attack he hasn't been able to deal with you, but I want you to know you've got me to contend with."

"You're my brother, Donald, not my father. Remember that." He was standing in her doorway and she jabbed her fingers into his chest, poking him, making him step back onto the cement front steps as she slammed the door with a reverberating crash.

"Out in a week! I want you home where you belong by this weekend!" he bellowed.

Mel turned around and leaned against the door, still shaking. Arms clasped tightly around her stomach, she slowly slid to the floor.

BUBBA GLANCED UP from pouring Henry's food when he heard the angry pounding. Setting the bag down on the kitchen counter, he jogged quickly into the foyer and pulled open the door.

Donnie walked in without bothering to say hello. "Bubba, who the hell has she been seeing?"

"Hello, Donnie."

"Who is he? What's the matter with her that she can't even use any common sense? I rented her that house so you could keep an eye on her, and now she's knocked up! Some good job you did!"

"Don, did Mel tell you why she had to get pregnant?"

"I don't know and I don't care."

"Come on, Don, stop behaving like an ass. This is Bubba, remember? Now sit down and give me five minutes."

Within three, Bubba was convinced Donnie just didn't *want* to understand.

"So why couldn't she find some guy and get married? Why did she have to do it all backward?"

"She wants to marry for love, Don, not just to have a father for her child."

"Hey, sometimes you just don't get choices in life. Sometimes you have to do what's *right*."

"That's strange, coming from you."

"Hey, Bubba, it's different for a man. But a girl like Mel—"

"She's twenty-six. I wouldn't call that being a girl."

"She's my *sister*, Bubba! Now you don't know anything about that, so I'd appreciate it if you'd keep your nose out of this!"

"Sorry. Anyway, Don," he said, glancing at his watch and making an effort to keep the sarcasm out of his voice, "It's been nice seeing you, but I have a date and I'm already late."

"You think this is just fine, don't you?"

"I think Mel made the choice that was right for her."

"God, Bubba, you're turning into a wimp! The next thing you know you'll be going over there and helping her make booties."

"Come on, Don, I'll walk you to the door."

"I gave her an ultimatum. She has to be out of the house by the weekend or I'll come and take her home myself."

"Fine. Now I'm really late and I'd appreciate it if you'd leave."

"You're taking her side, aren't you?"

"I think you're behaving like a fool."

"Then *you* help her out, *you* marry her and support someone else's brat! I don't know why having a kid was so important that she had to go and do it before she thought it through! I can't believe—"

"I know what you can't believe. Now I'm going to walk you out to your car."

Bubba heaved a sigh of relief as he watched Don drive away; then he turned and looked at Melanie's house.

He'd move her into his house today.

Chapter Ten

Mel was lying down on her bed, staring at the ceiling when Bubba walked in.

"You're still alive?" she asked sarcastically.

"I didn't tell him," Bubba replied. "You said you didn't want anyone to know. A deal's a deal."

She sighed. "Thank you. I'm sorry I snapped at you. Donnie just pushes all the right buttons and gets me all wound up."

He sat down on the bed. "I have a proposition to discuss with you."

"No, I won't move into your house."

His astonishment must have shown in his face because she smiled sadly. "Bubba, you've already put yourself on the line for me more than anyone I've ever known. I can't let you do any more."

"Where will you go?"

"I'm sure Alicia can let me sleep on her couch until I can rent an apartment."

He took one of her hands in his. "Listen to me a second. Haven't things been fine just the way they are? I don't want you somewhere where I can't check up on you and make sure you're okay."

"Bubba, this is not your concern."

"Come on, Mel, I think we're beyond this. It's my concern and you know it." When she didn't answer, he continued. "I've tried to tell you how I feel about you, but you keep pushing me away. The whole thing just sneaked up on me. It started out as friendship, but it's turning into something else."

She sat up and looked straight into his eyes. "I feel like I never gave you a choice in any of this. Like I took advantage of you."

"Yeah, and I really struggled."

She was silent for a moment, then said, "Okay," so quietly he thought for a moment he had to be hearing things.

"Okay? That's it?"

"Okay. But I don't want you to mention anything else about our relationship until after the baby is born. Nothing in my pregnancy was anything like I expected, so why should actually having a baby be any different?"

He was about to reply, but she shook her head.

"Wait until she's here, Bubba. It may be something you want nothing to do with."

"I want you—that's enough."

"No, it's not. If we were to get married now, I'd always wonder if it was me or the baby."

It was enough that she was moving in with him. The rest would come with time. "Okay. Fair enough. I'm going to call Terry and see if he can help us move. I don't want you doing any heavy lifting."

She surprised him then, putting her arms around him and hugging him tightly. He could feel the famil-

iar response in his body, just from the softness of her
skin, her touch, her own particular scent. But he was
careful to kiss her chastely on the forehead and smile
down at her.

TERRY WAS HOME, and the move took all of Sunday
even though half the furniture was left behind, since
it belonged to Donnie. In the end, when Mel dropped
the key in the mail to her brother along with a short,
terse note that didn't reveal she was staying with
Bubba, she felt as if she'd been set free. She wasn't
living under Donnie's roof anymore. She would never
accept anything from him again.

Living with Bubba was much the same as the
months he'd spent at her house. Now that she had her
energy back, she made him new kitchen curtains,
cleaned and repapered the shelves, cooked him meals.
Mel wanted to make sure he never regretted opening
his home to her, so she worked herself as hard as she
dared, trying to be a thoughtful guest.

He moved her bed into the spare bedroom, along
with the crib she'd purchased. That had been the
hardest part of moving, dismantling the nursery. She'd
cried as she'd taken down the ruffled curtains, packed
the stuffed animals into a big box, folded up the tiny
afghans and quilts. She was glad Donnie had never
seen it.

Once she was moved into the spare bedroom, she
began to prepare for the baby in earnest. She felt glued
to her sewing machine as she made a set of crib
bumpers and another quilt. Bubba brought home a
mobile made up of circus clowns one day, and she

hung it over the crib along with the dancing bears. She was intensely grateful to him for letting her set up the nursery in her bedroom. It helped her continue to see the baby as real, not something Donnie could take away from her.

Her older brother's suggestions chilled her. Bubba had told her Donnie knew about her medical condition, that he'd tried to explain why she'd chosen to get pregnant, but her brother still refused to understand. So Mel came to accept it. She decided she wouldn't go home for Christmas. Donnie would find some way to make things miserable, and she didn't want to put her parents through that.

As Christmas came closer, she shopped, wrapped presents and baked cookies for Bubba, but her heart wasn't really in any of it.

"NINE PEOPLE? Who's coming to dinner?" Mel asked as she pushed the cart down the aisle. It was the day before Christmas Eve, and they were stocking up for the holiday. Bubba was scanning the grocery list, trying to decipher her handwriting.

"You, me, my mother, and six very dear friends of mine." Bubba wrinkled his brow. "Mel, what does that say?"

She studied the list for a minute. "I think it says baking powder. I used the last we had in the chocolate-chip cookies."

"Does Alicia have a place to go?"

"She's meeting her mother in Austria. They're going skiing."

They shopped companionably, having done it together many times. They'd both agreed on a completely nontraditional menu: French onion soup, stuffed shrimp and a recipe Mel had pulled out of one of her cookbooks called "Mediterranean Vegetables." The pièce de résistance was going to be a trifle cake.

"You're sure everyone won't mind missing out on turkey or roast or something like that?" Mel asked later at the Santa Monica Fish Market.

Bubba shook his head. "Whatever we make will be fine with this crowd."

She wondered. She knew he was nervous about seeing his mother. She'd announced suddenly that she was going to be in town. Surprisingly, Mrs. Williams had bloomed after her divorce. There were a few painful years at first; then she'd gone back to school and had started to travel by herself. But her relationship with Bubba was still strained. Mel sometimes got the impression it was painful for her to look at him.

"We have to get a tree on the way home," Bubba reminded her as they were in the checkout line.

"I don't really care. Do you?" She knew he rarely put up a tree when he spent Christmas Day by himself, and she didn't want to make him work any harder on her account.

"We could set it up tonight." He was looking down at her, letting the final decision be hers alone. And for some strange reason, she sensed the answer was important to him.

"Okay." She made the effort to smile. "I'd like that."

"You know Henry will tear down all the ornaments, but it's the thought that counts."

That same evening, after Mel made grilled-cheese sandwiches and heated up a can of tomato soup, they began to decorate the tree. She watched suspiciously as Bubba unwrapped brand-new packages of Christmas lights and ornaments.

"How long has it been since you've had a tree?" she asked.

He shrugged. "I just got tired of all the old stuff."

They laughed and talked as the tree slowly filled with ornaments. It was impossible to stay depressed as the pine scent began to fill the house. Bubba had also insisted on buying extra greenery for the banister and the fireplace mantel, and Mel lost herself in decorating.

She'd always loved doing the house up at Christmas. It saddened her to see her old house, empty and silent, without any decorations or a tree in the big picture window in front. How could Donnie leave a house empty at Christmas?

Afterward, she made hot spiced cider and Bubba lit a fire. The lights on the tree flashed on and off in the darkened room.

"It's the prettiest tree I've ever seen," Mel said softly.

"That's what you say every year."

"And every year it's true." She was sitting slightly apart from Bubba on the sofa, wishing she had the right to curl up next to him and put her head on his shoulder. But she didn't.

"Watch Henry," Bubba said softly.

The cat had hidden underneath the coffee table while they'd decorated the tree, but now he slunk out slowly, his large belly close to the ground as he crept closer and closer to the tree.

Mel almost laughed, but Bubba signaled her to be quiet. As they watched, Henry circled the tree, eyeing it warily, then darted underneath it and began to paw at the lower branches, making them shake and the ornaments fly off.

"Now I understand why you said no glass ornaments," Mel said.

"Or tinsel. He ate some of yours last year, and I had to take him to the vet."

Henry merely watched both of them, his eyes glowing as he peered out from underneath the tree.

"He'll stay there all Christmas. He likes it because the tree is in a corner, so he feels he's completely surrounded.

"I think he just likes to mess around with plants," Mel replied. She'd had to hang most of her plants because Henry had the unfortunate habit of digging in the pots and tearing up the roots—not to mention chewing leaves.

"I'd like to give you your present privately if you wouldn't mind," Bubba said quietly, his eyes on the flashing lights. "Everyone will be here tomorrow night."

She was slightly startled. What could he have for her that he couldn't give her in public? But she managed to control her curiosity and nodded.

He brought the package downstairs from his bedroom. It was enormous, and he carried it as if it were heavy. Setting it down on the floor in front of her, he stepped back and looked down at her.

"Merry Christmas, Mel."

She felt queerly light-headed as she fumbled with the bright red bow, carefully untaped the candy-striped paper. She pushed it all away, revealing an enormous cardboard box.

"Is this like we used to do as kids when you opened one box and found another, then another, then another?" She made a quick joke to cover her nervousness.

"Take a look and see." Now *he* seemed to be the nervous one. Not able to stand the suspense a moment longer, she untaped the top of the box and pulled it open. It was padded with tissue paper, and she pulled it out until she uncovered— A cradle.

She felt as if all her breath had left her lungs and was lodged in her throat. She couldn't move, could only stare.

"I thought you could put it next to your bed."

"Oh, Bubba." The words were barely a whisper.

"That book the doctor recommended you read said they like to be rocked."

"Oh, Bubba. Did you make this?"

He seemed suddenly shy. "Terry's got a workshop in his garage. It didn't take that long."

But she could see the delicate pattern on the headboard, the graceful lines. It was beautiful dark oak, and she knew he had put his heart into making it special for her.

She was trying very hard not to cry. "Skip will love it."

"Well, I figure by the time she's three I'll make her a surfboard."

"You think it's going to be a girl?"

"I don't know, but I know you do."

"I'm joking, Bubba. I just want a healthy baby." She moved back up on the couch with him, her hand still touching the smooth finish of the cradle. Slowly, she took it out of the box and set it on the rug. Tentatively touching it, she watched as it rocked.

Turning toward him, her heart in her eyes, she put her arms around his neck and kissed him. It wasn't a friendly kiss, but a kiss meant to convey the depth of feeling she had for him.

As he started to kiss her back, he lowered her gently down on the couch.

"I SEE YOU, Henry. Don't even *think* about stealing one of those shrimp." Mel kept glancing at the cat lurking underneath the butcher-block table as she chopped vegetables, including onions for the soup. She'd started cooking early that morning, leaving Bubba asleep in bed.

She couldn't rationalize away what had happened last night. There was a powerful attraction between them. She'd wanted to be close to him, but each time she felt she was sliding closer and closer to the moment when she'd have to admit she loved him.

Not now. You have to give him more of a chance to make up his own mind—without all the emotional pressures. Her older sister Stef—the younger twin— had married her boyfriend right out of high school, when she'd found out she was pregnant. She could still remember the tension in the family, the strain of lies. "Molly was born early, she was premature." "Stef conceived on her honeymoon." "It's good to start a family right after marriage."

But nothing could make her forget the quiet despair on her sister's face when she'd come home, carrying her one-year-old daughter. The marriage was over. John had felt he'd been tied down before he was ready to settle down. It didn't matter that three years later Stef met a man at work who took one look at her and decided she was the woman he wanted to marry. She'd had it with men, but Roy had persisted, and now she was happily married and the mother of three children.

Not for me. I'd rather know what I'm going into right from the beginning. It seemed a long time ago that she'd come to Bubba's doorstep and asked him to get her pregnant. So much had happened. He'd said his feelings were slowly starting to change. But did he care for her? Or did he feel responsible? Though Bubba was a free spirit, he had an abiding sense of responsibility to his friends. She didn't want to be a "responsibility." She wanted to be loved for herself.

Come on, Mel. You don't spend your evenings working on a cradle because it's a responsibility. That was a loving thing to do. Quit being so damn defensive and give Bubba a chance. She wanted to. Oh, how she wanted to. She'd lain awake nights in bed, thinking it was ridiculous to go on this way, living underneath the same roof and accepting the quiet tension between them. They covered it well, with jokes and laughter, but it erupted at times, moments they couldn't joke away or control. Last night had been one of those moments, and it had been wonderful.

He'd been infinitely careful with her. She hadn't been aware that he'd read several of the pregnancy books her doctor had recommended until he assured her they wouldn't harm the baby. "We have ways," he whispered in her ear. And though she'd felt fat and frumpy the afternoon they'd been shopping for groceries, that night she believed she was beautiful.

She saw the chubby white paw a second before it swiped up on the table.

"Henry!" The cat thundered away, and she had to laugh. Whoever it was who had written about "little cat feet" hadn't met this guy. Feeling immediately guilty that she'd yelled at him, she took two shrimp out of the colander and walked into the living room.

Henry was glowering underneath the tree behind several gaily wrapped packages.

"I can see you, Hen, and I'm sorry. Come back into the kitchen and I'll put these in your bowl."

Before the sentence was finished, the cat had darted out, smelling the shellfish. He marched into the kitchen with her, his tail waving, and she plopped the food into his dish. He attacked it, making little growling noises in the back of his throat.

"You're giving shrimp to Minnie the Moocher?" Bubba asked.

She turned around, the butcher block at her back. He looked as if he'd just rolled out of bed. His hair was rumpled and his face still looked sleepy. Dressed casually in a pair of jeans, he looked relaxed and happy.

"It was that or risk having my legs slashed."

Bubba walked lazily over to the refrigerator and took out the carton of orange juice. "Tell me what to do or I'll get out of your way."

"If you sauté the onions, I can start making the trifle."

"That's right—stick me with the dangerous job." But he was smiling.

They worked companionably for almost two hours, talking and laughing, discussing anything but what had happened last night. It was as if, Mel thought, neither of them really knew what to say. She wondered if he would expect her simply to move into his room.

No, not Bubba. Stop giving him all those machismo qualities just because you're nervous.

By late afternoon the meal was under control, and she went upstairs to change. Bubba had insisted they both dress up, so after her shower she slipped on a light wool dress in a soft rose shade. It was obviously a maternity dress. She'd bought only three, preferring to spend her time in jeans into which she'd sewn a maternity panel. At the store, she wore a loose skirt with a variety of her hand-knit sweaters. She found it was a good way of helping customers see all the various options they had when dressing in her creations.

She left her hair loose and applied makeup sparingly. There really was a glow about her. During the first three months, she'd wondered what all those people were talking about when they said pregnant women bloomed. Now she could see what they meant. She finally felt pretty again.

She slipped on her hose, and flats, then walked over to her closet and took out the package she'd wrapped for Bubba. It was a sweater she'd spent two months making, thick and patterned. She could picture him wearing it during his winter walks on the beach. Of deep, blue-gray wool, it would set off his blond coloring perfectly.

She could hear the shower running, so she slipped downstairs and put his present behind several of the bigger packages.

By seven that evening, she and Bubba were sitting on the couch, watching the tree lights wink on and off. When the doorbell sounded, Bubba got up off the couch.

"I'll get it."

Mel leaned her head back and closed her eyes. Though her energy had peaked in the past month, there were still moments when she felt tired. Maybe she could sneak away and take a nap sometime during the evening; then she could make it to midnight, when they traditionally opened presents.

"Melanie?"

She thought she was dreaming, hearing the familiar voice, but when she opened her eyes and turned her head around, she saw her mother and father standing in back of the sofa, concerned expressions on both their faces. She stood up slowly, watching their reactions as they took in her physical appearance. Bubba was right behind them, his eyes warm, reassuring.

"Mother, what are you—" Her throat tightened up and she couldn't get the words out of her mouth.

"Bubba asked us to come." Her mother was rushing her words, as if she, too, were nervous. She was holding a red-and-white package in her hands and was slowly crushing the small box. "He told Sandy everything, and she sat us down and explained."

"Did she explain to Donnie?" She glanced wildly at Bubba. "If he's coming here tonight—"

"Donnie won't be here," Bubba said.

There was an awkward moment of silence; then her mother walked slowly around the sofa until she stood in front of her. Though Mel searched her mother's eyes carefully for signs of condemnation, she saw nothing but quiet concern.

"Oh, Melanie, why didn't you tell me everything right from the start?"

She could feel some of the isolation that had enveloped her for so many weeks begin to melt away.

"You aren't upset?"

"Upset?" Her father finally spoke. His voice was slightly gruff, and he ran his hand over his balding head, a gesture she knew he used only when he was nervous. "After Sandy told us why you decided to go ahead, we thought you made a good choice."

"You did?" Her voice sounded strange to her ears.

"Melanie, I knew how much you were looking forward to a family," her mother said quietly. Mel quickly searched her mother's lined face for signs of displeasure but found only solicitude in her brilliant blue eyes. "Why would I condemn you for wanting a child?"

"Then you don't mind if...if I'm not—"

"There is no such thing as an illegitimate child in my family," her father stated firmly. "And you, young lady, have been worrying your mother for the past two weeks." He glanced at Bubba. "I think we should all have a drink and start dinner, don't you?"

Mel could only stare. For just a second, she had glimpsed her father again as she remembered him in earlier times, showing his old, quiet strength and compassion.

"What would you like?" Bubba asked.

"The damn doctor has me on a restricted diet," her father grumbled.

"A little wine?" Bubba offered.

"Hell, yes! It's not every day I have a grandchild coming into the world."

"Oh, Daddy. Thank you," Mel breathed quietly. Then she looked into her mother's eyes. "Oh, Mama."

Her mother's arms wrapped around her, and she tried very hard not to cry.

CHRISTMAS EVE was a smashing success. Bubba's mother arrived soon after, and fell right into animated conversation with Mel's parents. When the doorbell pealed again, Mel answered and was delighted to find her sister Sandy with her husband, Bill, and their two children at the door.

"Mad at me?" Bubba whispered later as they both went into the kitchen to bring out the dinner.

"No." She gave his arm a quick squeeze. "I'm glad you got to them before Donnie did."

"I called Sandy as soon as Don left my house. I didn't think you'd want him to tell them."

"What happened?"

Bubba grinned. "Sandy called me afterward to tell me. I wish I'd been there. Donnie exploded in the door in one of his righteous wraths, told your parents, and your father looked up over his paper and said, 'Yes, Don, your mother and I are fully aware of what Melanie's up to. Are you staying for dinner?'"

She started to laugh. "I can just see Daddy doing that!"

"I always liked his sense of humor."

They lingered over dessert and coffee. Melanie watched Bubba with her niece and nephew. Ten-year-old Jennifer and seven-year-old Michael behaved like absolute angels after Bubba promised them he'd take them to the beach Christmas Day.

"You'll be staying the night, then?" Mel asked her mother.

The older woman shook her head. "Bubba booked us rooms at the Holiday Inn right by the beach. I've been looking forward to a little vacation with your father, and Bubba was kind enough to suggest we come."

Melanie could just picture the two of them together, walking along the beach. Her father would buy some ridiculous hat and wear it just to annoy her mother. They would stop for lunch, and he would try to get away with ordering something not on his diet, but she would quietly restrain him.

She had missed them terribly. It had always been her plan to tell them at Christmastime, but when Donnie had broken into her life and disrupted everything, she had lost her confidence.

After dinner, Bubba and Bill unloaded the presents from both cars and they all sat in the living room. Bubba lit a fire and put on an album of Christmas carols. Mel popped popcorn and played with the children. They were excited, asking every few minutes what time it was and if they *please* couldn't open just one present.

Bubba entertained them by telling them what he had planned for the following day. It gave Mel a chance to sit with her mother and sister and catch them up on everything. They listened as Mel described her medical care, how her pregnancy was progressing, how she had felt so far.

"I was sick as a dog with Jennifer but not as much with Michael," Sandy told her, keeping one eye on her children at all times. Bubba had taken Michael out to the backyard because he wanted to see the hot tub, and they were visible through the sliding glass door.

"I was sick with all five of you. Especially the twins," her mother confessed.

"How could you go through it so many times?" Mel asked, totally in awe. Pregnancy made her see her mother in an entirely new way.

"You just do, and it's only bad in the beginning." Her mother studied her thoughtfully. "Did you tell your doctor twins run in my side of the family?"

For a moment Mel was totally stunned. *Twins.* There had been times in her pregnancy she was sure she couldn't cope with one child, let alone two.

"I'll phone her next week."

At midnight they opened their presents. She could tell Bubba was pleased with his sweater. He pulled it over his head immediately, even though the living room was warm. Mel's mother gave her what she always gave her at Christmas—a pretty nightgown and scented soap. But Mel's lips curved into a smile—this year it was a maternity nightgown, with a button front. She also gave her a cross-stitch sampler to hang in the nursery, with tiny bears and colorful balloons on it.

The living room was completely awash in wrapping paper when, an hour after midnight, Bubba and Mel stood on the front steps and waved as their guests made their way to their respective cars.

"They'll be back for brunch tomorrow, but I said anyone who showed up before noon wouldn't get anything to eat!" Bubba yawned. "I'm going to get some sleep. You must be exhausted."

"Did your mom have a good time?"

"Yeah, she did. I know she loved seeing your folks again."

As they slowly climbed the stairs, Mel wished she could simply follow Bubba into his bedroom. After last night. *No, don't take anything for granted.*

They stopped in front of his door, and he slowly pulled her into his arms.

"I'll see you in the morning, Mel." Was it her imagination, or was there the slightest tone of regret in his voice?

"Thank you for tonight, Bubba. It meant so much to me being with my family."

He drew her into his arms, his chin resting on the top of her head. "It wasn't completely for you. It was kind of a fantasy of mine."

She was silent, waiting for him to continue.

"All those times when I used to hang out at your house and talk to your dad, I promised myself that someday I'd have him and your mom over to my house. And it wouldn't be like the house I grew up in—it would be exactly like it was tonight."

Her eyes stung as she thought of all the Christmases he'd missed. On the surface, everything had probably been there—the tree, the presents, his parents—but it had been nothing like the holidays she'd enjoyed.

"I'm glad it finally happened."

They stood perfectly still, their bodies close together, neither wanting to make the first move to break apart.

"I suppose I should let you go," he said finally.

"I suppose so." She tightened her grip around his waist. She was shameless, but she didn't care.

"I think you'd get more sleep if you went into your own bedroom," he said softly. "Being the maniac that I am, I won't be held accountable for my actions." She could hear just a hint of humor in his voice.

"Being the maniac that I am, I probably won't take your advice."

"I'm glad." Slowly, ever so slowly, he stepped back slightly and lowered his lips to hers. As he started to kiss her, she felt everything around her begin to fade away. There was no reality except the man in her arms.

Chapter Eleven

She'd never enjoyed a holiday more. Her parents stayed for three days, before driving home. Her mother made her promise to call every couple of days and said she wanted to come to dinner sometime in January. Bubba asked Mel to go with him to a New Year's Eve party at Terry's house, and when midnight rolled around, he kissed her. It was only when she stepped back that she noticed several people staring at them.

It had probably looked funny—Bubba kissing an obviously pregnant woman most of Terry's friends had never seen before.

After the holidays they settled into a very comfortable routine, and it seemed to Mel she'd never lived anywhere but in Bubba's house. He watched her every move, made sure she drank her milk, exercised and didn't overexert herself.

Her love deepened, but she remained silent. It was only at night, in Bubba's embrace, that she dared express what was deep within her heart. Some nights they didn't make love. They just talked quietly, wrapped in each other's arms. When they were intimate, Bubba was especially tender and gentle, and each time Melanie felt herself falling deeper and deeper in love.

Their time together flew by. One day in January, she was lying out on a chaise near the hot tub. Her knitting needles and yarn were in a tote by her side, but Mel simply lay in the sun and relaxed, with Henry at her feet.

She felt good. Really good. At peace with herself.

Bubba cared. She knew that now. Though neither of them talked about marriage, she knew the depth of his feeling for her. After Christmas Eve, she had simply moved into his bedroom. If she couldn't give him anything else, she knew he loved waking up with her at his side in the morning. And she loved to fall asleep in his arms.

She turned her head as she heard the glass door slide open. Bubba appeared, dressed casually in a pair of gray slacks and the sweater she'd given him for Christmas.

"You're sure you don't want to come with me? Mom won't mind."

She shook her head. It was rare that Mrs. Williams asked her son to lunch. Mel didn't want to intrude on the beginnings of a tenuous relationship. It seemed his mother was trying. She'd spent Christmas Eve with them. She'd dropped by one evening after that. Now lunch. Something was going on, and Mel didn't want to intrude.

"Eat a dessert for me," she said, patting her stomach.

"Will you stop worrying about gaining so much weight. You're eating for a future surfing champion."

She laughed. Bubba insisted his child would love the ocean as he did, and she knew their baby would. How could she miss, with her parents being the outdoors buffs they were?

"Cheesecake—it's my favorite."

He smiled, leaned over and gave her a kiss. Within minutes, she heard the sound of his car starting up. She closed her eyes and turned her face into the sunshine.

"MOTHER, JUST TELL ME what's bothering you." Bubba shifted uncomfortably in his chair. Something was wrong. Lunch had been a disaster, his mother so obviously nervous she could barely eat a mouthful.

"Robert, I asked you to lunch today because I have something to tell you."

"You're getting married." His mother had remarried once after the divorce but been single within three years.

"No, I'll never get married again."

He could detect real pain in the depth of her light blue eyes, and suddenly it unnerved him. "Are you all right?"

She patted his arm awkwardly. "I'm fine." Intimacy was difficult between them, old habits hard to break.

He sat back in his chair and stared at her, glad Mel had decided to remain at home. What the hell was going on?

She took a deep breath. "I should have told you this years ago, but I thought you suffered enough when your father and I got divorced."

Your father. For as long as he could remember, she'd never referred to his father as my husband or even Harold. It had always been "your father."

She looked terribly vulnerable, and in a completely spontaneous gesture, he took one of her hands in both of his.

"C'mon, Mom, spit it out. Nothing can be that bad."

Her eyes were anguished. "Oh, Robert, he's not your father."

He listened in stunned silence as she told him of the brief love affair that had resulted in his birth, of her decision to get a divorce. And what Harold had done, the ultimatum he'd given her because he'd been so very, very bitter: she could leave, but he'd make sure she'd never see her child again.

He listened, his chest feeling tighter and tighter. When she finished telling him the entire story, he asked the one question he had to.

"Does my real father know about me?"

She nodded her head.

"Do I know him?"

"No."

His hand tightened around hers. "Will you give me his address?" He had to know. Suddenly all the times he'd felt as if he were not quite his father's son made sense. They had never been alike.

Her eyes filled with tears, she nodded her head.

HE LAY IN BED with Melanie that night, staring at the ceiling, trying to make sense of his world. In the space of an afternoon, it had been rocked right off its foundation.

Santa Barbara. Ninety miles up the coast. Some of the most beautiful beaches in the world. His father. Jonathan Mills. Just a name on a scrap of paper, but it was all he had.

He remembered all the times he'd attempted to be close to his father and the countless little ways he'd been pushed away. Bubba had been eight years old when Donnie had asked him over to play, and the moment he'd pushed the door open at the Randell household, he'd felt the warmth.

It had been so lacking in his own life, he'd embraced this new family, watching, fascinated, as they shouted and argued, loved and *cared* for each other. And every evening after he went home, he ate dinner at a table with his silent parents and wished for a brother like Donnie, just so he wouldn't feel so alone.

Mel shifted in her sleep and sighed. She kicked off the covers all the time now, claiming she was too warm. He studied the smooth swell of her belly, the taut lines of her breasts. Gently, so as not to wake her, he placed his hand over her stomach.

She sighed and moved closer to his touch.

For the first time, Bubba thought about their baby as an actual child. Pregnancy was such an abstract idea. It was hard to believe Mel was going to have a baby—*they* were going to have a baby.

He thought of his mother. She must have been miserable. If her husband had given her an ultimatum like that when she wanted to leave him, how supportive could he have been while she was pregnant? So much of the quiet tension between his parents made sense now: the way his father—stepfather—had watched his mother, never let her out of his sight. The slightly cowed expression she'd always worn. Even the way they'd stayed as far apart as possible—his stepfather in his office, his mother in her house.

Their lives had both been over, and they'd known it.

"Bubba?" Mel's voice was sleepy.

He realized he'd been squeezing her stomach slightly, and he dropped his hand, ashamed of waking her. He wanted to ask her to take him in her arms and tell him she loved him, but he didn't want her to think he was weak. So he remained silent.

"What's wrong?"

"Nothing. I'm just tense."

"Do you want me to rub your back?"

"No. Go back to sleep."

He could feel her eyes on him, then he felt her hand reach out and brush his hair back from his forehead.

"Did you have a good time with your mom?"

His eyes stung. Her touch was so tender, so knowing. Mel never damanded an answer; she simply asked the right questions or listened—and waited for him to tell her. But he couldn't. Not yet.

"You know Mom," he said roughly.

"I think she tried very hard, Bubba. I always—"
She stopped in midsentence, and he glanced quickly at

her face. She had the strangest expression, and for a moment, sheer, unreasoning terror washed over him.

Something's wrong—

"Bubba," she whispered. "Oh, Bubba, she's moving! I can feel her, right inside me! Oh, my God, she's moving!"

She groped for his hand, pressed it against her stomach. He couldn't feel anything but her intense excitement.

"What does it feel like?" He was curious and scared at the same time. There was someone in there.

"Like—" she wrinkled her face in concentration "—like a little butterfly. Like she's turning over. Oh, Bubba, do you feel it?"

"I can't tell if it's you or her."

"Maybe she'll do it again."

They waited, lying side by side in the darkness, but nothing happened. Then Mel said quietly, "There she goes again."

He gathered her into his arms, holding her tightly against him. He could feel her heart beating rapidly. He needed to hold her, needed to let her know how very special she was to him.

He felt her lips brush against his ear. "I love you, Bubba. I shouldn't tell you, but I've loved you for a long time."

"Me, too." It was all he could get past the sudden tightness in his chest.

NOW THAT THERE WERE NO SECRETS between them, each day flowed into the next and Mel really began to enjoy her pregnancy. The baby had become real to her.

With just the slightest, sweetest fluttering movement, she suddenly became a person.

"Danielle. I like the name Danielle." They were lying on the couch, watching the rain patter against the sliding glass door.

"What happened to poor old Skip?" Bubba hugged her playfully.

"Only if it's a boy."

Bubba tickled her ear. "Did the doctor hear any multiple heartbeats?" He teased her about twins constantly. "The deal's off if you have a litter," he announced over breakfast one day. "It'll be settled fair and square—one for you and one for me." At her horrified look, he'd laughed and reached over to tweak her hair.

"Everything's fine. There's only one heartbeat in there that she knows of."

"Danielle and Skip. I like that combination."

"Danielle. Or maybe Alexandra," Mel said.

"Alexandra sounds like a Russian princess."

"Please don't use that word in this house." They both laughed, remembering Phillip and the unfortunate Joel.

"Now there you go. If it's boy twins, we can call them Phil and Joel. They'll grow up to be musicians, not surfers. Those are good musician names."

"Oh, please. Why don't we get a kitten and call it Skip? You seem to have a fixation on that name."

"Hey, I like Danielle. The kids at school can call her Dani."

"Finally something we agree on." She heaved a mock sigh of relief. "But what if it's a boy? Robert junior? Bobby?"

"Nope," Bubba said quickly. "I'd want him to have a name of his own. That baby book said you can give a kid a complex by saddling it with someone else's name."

Mel started to laugh. "What was the name of that guy on those old Gidget movies you used to make me watch? What was it?"

He didn't answer.

She tickled his ribs. "Moondoggie! That's it! Skip and Moondoggie! They're unisex names; we have two picked just in case. Bubba, I can tell you don't like it."

"The kids will call him Moon for short."

She was laughing so hard now that tears were rolling down her cheeks. "Can you see me on the front steps—'Moon, Skip, you two get in here this minute!'" She couldn't stop laughing and her stomach was starting to hurt.

"Moon just doesn't sound right."

"Didn't Frank Zappa name his daughter Moon Unit? I think it's pretty distinctive."

He growled deep in his throat, then rolled her carefully over on her back and nipped her neck gently. "If you're not careful I'll moon you."

"It'll be nothing I haven't seen before." She shrieked as he started to tickle her.

SEVERAL EVENINGS LATER, he broached what was on his mind.

"I think we need to go on a honeymoon, Mel."

She looked over at him, the sweater she had been knitting completely forgotten. He'd captured her attention.

"What?"

"Now, before you say anything, hear me out. I thought we could take a long weekend and drive up the coast. Nothing fancy, just something a little romantic."

She was bristling slightly, so he could tell she was pleased. Mel could sometimes get a little prickly when she was feeling deep emotion.

"When did you think this up?" Her question was abrupt, but her eyes were dancing with happiness.

"Well, since you refuse to make an honest man of me..."

"Bubba, we've been through this a million times. Henry is going to remain the fattest thing in white in Santa Monica."

"Will you cut that out!"

"I can't get married looking this hideous."

"You look beautiful to me."

"We could elope."

"Nope, that's not good enough. I thought we could get married in the backyard."

"Someone will mistake me for a great white shark and shoot to kill."

"You could wear a red dress."

"And look like a tomato? No thank you."

He knew her fears were lurking just behind the bantering. Mel still wanted them to wait. She wanted him to have time to get to know his child and see if being a father was an experience he wanted. But he knew, now more than ever, that he didn't want any life but the one he could share with her.

"We could sleep in, make love, eat croissants, order lunch in, make love—"

"Then why go to Santa Barbara?"

"Well, we might take a walk or two. You know what honeymoons are for."

"I think we've practiced enough." She was grinning.

"This is really important to me, Mel. I'd like to drive up this Thursday night."

"I'd love to. You know, if I finish that sundress with the stripes, I can camouflage myself as a beach ball."

"Mel!"

FRIDAY MORNING he asked her to stay at the hotel while he ran a quick errand. He made sure she was settled in by the pool with a fat paperback before he got into the car and headed toward town.

He'd always liked Santa Barbara. There was an ordinance that prohibited buildings from towering too high, so the city had resisted that overdeveloped, crowded look so many Southern California areas fell prey to. The main architecture was Spanish stucco with deep red tile, and flowers bloomed everywhere.

He'd already asked for directions by phone and set up an appointment with Jonathan Mills. He had to know who his father was. His mother had said he'd kept track of Bubba from the moment he was born. Bubba had been relieved when he'd learned from Mr. Mills's secretary that he would see him.

Father or not, he still could have refused.

His stomach seemed to tighten as he found the building, parked and walked inside and up the stairs to the second floor. Glancing at the office door and recognizing the name, Bubba pushed it gently open and walked inside.

Within minutes he was in his father's office.

The man behind the desk stood up as he entered. Bubba recognized the eyes first—the same dark blue-gray. His blond hair was thinning, his face deeply tanned and etched with strong lines from a life outdoors. It was like looking in a mirror, seeing what he'd be like twenty-five years from now. Though the resemblance wasn't exact, there was enough that he had no doubt this man was the father he'd searched for, unknowingly, all his life.

They stood still, staring awkwardly at each other, until Jonathan spoke. "I canceled my other appointments today. I thought we could take a drive out to my house and talk."

"Did my mother call you?"

"She let me know she told you." Bubba could feel keen eyes taking him in, and for once in his life he didn't feel he was lacking.

He sat down slowly in one of the chairs by the desk.

"Would you like a drink?" his father asked.

"Just Coke, thank you." It was so difficult, trying to find the words. He didn't really know what to say.

As his father walked over to the built-in bar, Bubba quickly scanned the office. Done in cool, muted shades of green and blue, with large lithographs of ocean creatures on the walls, it was an office in which he felt comfortable.

As his father handed him a glass, he suddenly realized he had no idea what the man did.

"What do you do?"

Jonathan couldn't seem to stop staring at him. "I work for the government. I help them set up programs to prevent environmental destruction of the ocean."

Bubba felt as if all the pieces of a gigantic jigsaw puzzle were slowly falling into place. He felt his body start to relax, let go of the tension he'd been holding in since his mother had made her quiet confession. He understood this man. On a deeper level, they were committed to the same things.

"I build houses," he said quietly. "Someday I want to construct buildings that are environmentally sound."

There was a gleam of something—pride?—in his father's eyes as he continued to study him.

"I surf, too," Bubba said.

At that, Jonathan smiled. "I used to, when I was your age." He glanced out the huge glass window and said quietly, "I met your mother at the beach."

Bubba put his glass down, his hands were starting to shake. This was what he'd really come for. What had happened?

"She wasn't the woman you grew up with. She was much more alive."

It was hard to picture his mother younger, freer. He had always seen her with that slightly worried expression, the frightened eyes and tense mouth.

"I knew she was married, but I couldn't seem to help myself. I always regretted the pain I caused her."

"How did Harold find out?" It had been so easy to stop thinking about that grim man as his father.

"He was sterile. They'd tried to start a family for years. When she became pregnant, he knew it wasn't—couldn't have been—his."

Bubba didn't know what to say.

"She loved you very much. I understood her decision. Your stepfather had money; he planned to retain custody of you by questioning whether your mother was morally fit to raise you. He was an extremely bitter man—about his own inadequacies more than anything else."

"My mother told me you knew who I was. Did you ever see me when I was growing up?"

"She sent me pictures." He opened the drawer and pulled out a scrapbook, then handed it to Bubba.

He settled it in his lap and began to turn the pages. Every school picture. Copies of report cards. Letters. There were manila envelopes full of letters. The newspaper clipping when he'd won a local surfing contest. The acceptance letter from his college.

"I knew of you, but I didn't know you. I had hoped that someday you might see it in your heart to come see me. But I left the decision as to whether you should be told to your mother."

Bubba closed the scrapbook. It was too much, all at once. "Can I keep this for a week or so, mail it back to you?"

He nodded, then handed Bubba one of his business cards.

"Did you ever get married?"

"Once. It lasted eight years. I did a disservice to Ann, marrying her when there was only one woman I ever wanted."

He stopped talking, and Bubba sensed his father was lost in his memories for a few moments. Then his face changed, cleared, and he stood up.

"I'd like to show you my home. My housekeeper has lunch waiting."

Bubba nodded, not trusting himself to speak.

IT WAS LIKE ONE of the houses he dreamed of building, all wood and glass, overlooking the Pacific. They sat out on the patio, and once lunch was served the housekeeper discreetly vanished.

And they began to talk. There were awkward attempts at first, embarrassed questions. But there was such a deep, common well of similarity to draw from.

Bubba was achingly glad that he *liked* his father. Strangely enough, at his worst moments with Harold, he'd fantasized he was adopted, never dreaming how close to the truth he was.

When he glanced at his watch, he was startled to see it was almost one o'clock. Mel would be wondering where he was.

"There's someone I'd like you to meet if you wouldn't mind."

Jonathan seemed more relaxed. "You have me for the rest of the day."

"Can I use your phone?"

He had Mel paged at the pool, but there was no response. Then he called their room, and she picked up on the second ring.

"Mel? I'm sorry I'm late."

"That's okay. I was taking a nap."

"There's something I'd like you to do for me. Something really important." Quickly he outlined his plan, giving her Jonathan's address, asking her to take a taxi to the house and meet him there.

She agreed, and he hung up the phone and joined his father out back.

Half an hour later, he heard the sound of a car pulling into the driveway. Excusing himself, he ran around front and met Mel. He watched her as she stepped out of the cab. She was dressed in one of his favorite dresses, a turquoise crinkled-cotton creation. She hadn't belted it, and the gentle wind molded it to the ripening curves of her figure.

"This way, Mel."

He could sense she knew this was important to him. Though he was almost bursting with impatience, he led her around the house, past the brilliantly blossoming flowers to the patio in back.

He kept his arm around her shoulders to steady her and heard her sharply indrawn breath as Jonathan stood up and smiled. So he hadn't been imagining it—the resemblance was there.

"Father, this is Melanie Randell, the woman I'm going to marry. Mel, this is my father, Jonathan Mills."

THEY SPENT THE REST of Friday with Bubba's father, then Saturday and early Sunday they strolled through Santa Barbara, sitting out in cafés and walking along the beaches. Mel pretended she was married to Bubba. It wasn't too hard, as everyone treated them that way.

She bought a stuffed otter for the nursery at one of the bookstores they browsed through, and Bubba bought several tiny silk-screen T-shirts. He also bought an album of ocean sounds.

"They say a baby can hear in the womb," he said at breakfast Sunday morning.

"Who is they, Dr. Spock?" she teased.

"I think we should play it tonight and see if we get a response."

"She can start surfing right now. She's surrounded by water."

He was amazing. He'd read more of the books than she had and was all ready to begin Lamaze classes when they returned home. Though she was still frightened by what lay ahead of them, Bubba's enthusiasm was too genuine to be faked. She knew he was looking forward to the birth.

"They say that sometimes if a man sees a woman give birth, he never wants to have sex with her again," she remarked as they drove home that afternoon.

"Not a chance. You're not getting rid of me that easily. When do the classes start?"

"The nurse said we should come in around the beginning of my seventh month. We've got a way to go yet."

"But don't you have to start practicing sooner than that?"

She'd never have believed it if the evidence wasn't staring her in the face every day. Bubba was so happy about this baby. She was, too, when she wasn't scared about what was going to happen when she finally went into labor. It scared her, that unknown journey.

But it can't be that bad—not with Bubba. Refusing to think about what she had absolutely no control over, she closed her eyes and leaned her head against his shoulder.

As Mel slept and Bubba drove, he let the hypnotic rhythm of watching the road take over, let his thoughts drift. They drifted to his father, to the entire weekend, to his finally putting the last piece of the puzzle in place.

They had talked about so much, as if their feelings had been bottled up all those years and finally let loose. And Jonathan had told him, before Mel arrived, of what it had been like to live an enormous part of his life on the sidelines—only to watch and never really participate.

"There will never be anything in my life that will make up for the time I couldn't spend with you or your mother. That is the deepest regret of my life." His eyes had been sad as he'd spoken, the weariness of years and years etched into the lines in his face. He had spoken of all the tiny things he had missed rather than the standard accomplishments. It hadn't been the high-school graduation as much as a quiet dinner with his real family. Or a day at the beach, a drive on Sunday.

Jonathan had missed it all, simply receiving his pictures and clippings. Toward the end of their lunch, he had said those words to Bubba that would be etched into his memory forever: "The deepest regret of my life…"

Mel shifted in her sleep and he tightened his arm around her shoulders. Expert at steering with one hand, he drove carefully in the slower lane of traffic, needing to touch her. He wanted to be close to Mel, but she still possessed that basic fear. He knew she was afraid she'd trapped him.

Her stand at independence covered what Bubba sensed was a deep fear—of being hurt, vulnerable. Of taking advantage of a friendship that was so very special.

Glancing at her golden head, he nuzzled his cheek against the softness of her hair, then returned his attention to the road.

Mel, you've got to understand. It turned into something better than friendship for me. And I know it's true for you, if you'd just admit it. This has nothing to do with being trapped, being obligated.

He couldn't pinpoint the exact moment. His feelings had grown and grown, and he'd *always* loved Mel, so when that love had stretched to encompass a completely different dimension, it had taken him a little time to understand. Now he knew, and the knowledge that she could walk out of his life because of a mistaken sense of duty made him understand his father's pain all the more poignantly.

And it's not only because of the baby, Mel. It's wanting to wake up every morning and start my days by seeing your face on the pillow next to mine. It's all the jokes we share and the way I can look across the room and smile and know what you're thinking. It's walks on the beach in the winter being the best thing in the world. It's going to bed at night and touching you, having you next to me underneath the covers and talking. Making love. It's wanting to share things with you first, and sometimes with no one else.

Though he was looking forward to their child's birth, a part of him was scared—for Mel and what she would go through, for the changes it would bring in their relationship. Would she move out? Would she attempt to make a break, not wanting to take advantage of him in her own mind? Would he be able to convince her that nothing was more important than staying together?

Mel shifted slightly in her sleep, and he tightened his grip around her shoulders for just a second. He glanced at the smoothness of her cheek, the soft smudge of her eyelashes. Then he returned his attention to the road once again.

Take it a day at a time. Remember Henry. He sits underneath those bushes and waits for those birds for a long time.

"You'll stay with me, Mel," he said softly to her sleeping form. "I'm not going to give you up now that I've really found you. And someone has to help you watch over Skip."

It's going to be me, he thought contentedly. Nothing could change something that felt so right. Mel would come around. Time and love were both on his side.

Chapter Twelve

Fat.

She'd thought she knew what the word meant, but the third trimester convinced Mel that all the rest had been a dress rehearsal.

She didn't feel fat. She felt obese, gargantuan, hideous, corpulent, bulky, massive, huge, immense, enormous, stupendous, monstrous, colossal, lumbering, unwieldy, whopping, bloated.

But not fat.

The first thing that depressed her was not being able to sleep on her stomach. The second thing was how much weight she was gaining. Though she'd followed the doctor's diet as carefully as possible, she seemed to puff up overnight, like bread dough left out to rise. The morning she discovered a slight double chin she cried for an hour.

But the realization that she had to waddle to get around was Mel's total undoing. Everything was different. The way she walked with her legs far apart, the way she had to get out of chairs or up off the floor after her breathing exercises. Her body felt different.

Her hips didn't move anymore when she walked, but her belly seemed to roll from side to side.

She couldn't cross her legs, couldn't jog around the block, couldn't even manage a brisk walk. Having always been a physically active woman, she felt the loss of movement as a personal loss of freedom.

Stupid little things set her off into tears. Alicia took her for a manicure and pedicure, but afterward Mel realized she couldn't see her feet.

The slight movements that had brought her such joy now seemed to batter and bruise her. The baby was terribly active, moving constantly. She was positive she could feel tiny feet pummeling her rib cage and up underneath her swollen breasts.

Most of all, she resented the invasion of her privacy, the way people thought that because she was pregnant they were welcome to touch her and offer various opinions and personal comments.

"Oh, it's a boy. They're always active."

"You're carrying it all out in front—a boy."

"My mother looked just like that when she had my sister."

"Eight months? Aren't you big!"

"Well you certainly eat for two!"

Nothing she tried made her happy. The hints in women's magazines were laughable. She felt like a whale, and even whales probably had more fun than she did. At least they could swim around and play in the ocean. And the ones she'd seen with Bubba off Catalina were gray—a slimming color.

Thank God for Bubba. She wasn't sure if she would have continued with her Lamaze classes without his calming presence. The first night they had class, one of the pregnant women kept staring at her. Mel tried not to stare back, but she was conscious of the woman's eyes on her the entire time. Before class was over, she sidled up to Mel and said, "Are you having twins or what?"

She'd cried all the way out to the car, all the way home. Nothing Bubba could say could shake the feeling she had that she was the fattest pregnant woman who had ever walked the face of the earth.

What had she done wrong? She'd followed the diet, jogged until she was uncomfortable, then walked with Bubba every night. But she refused to waddle.

Yet she did. She waddled through her days and slept restlessly through her nights. She didn't even feel right about curling up next to Bubba for comfort, since the baby kicked so hard she kept him awake.

See, even now the baby is coming between us.

He never complained, never hesitated to comfort her in any way he could. The more he did for her the worse she felt, because she knew she was being a terrible crab and, worse, a complete baby herself.

Why was something that should have been so wonderful so horrible?

Joanie and Alicia continued to stop by, but toward the end of her pregnancy, Mel started to pretend she was asleep when anyone visited. She was tired of pretending she was happy being pregnant. Nothing had prepared her for the reality of what was happening to her body.

Her worst, most private fears she kept to herself. She couldn't shake the feeling that something was wrong with the baby because she'd blown up so quickly. And her due date had already passed. But as her monthly checks with the doctor became weekly, nothing abnormal turned up. She was just enormous.

And Bubba. Why should any man on earth find the world's largest pregnant woman attractive? She worried about losing her sex appeal. It wasn't hard when all you wanted to do was plant yourself in a chair in front of a fan, put your feet up and forget.

She could feel the slight contractions ripple through her body, knew it was her body's way of preparing for delivery. If she thought the sight of her waddling through the house must be off-putting, she couldn't wait for the birth. Bubba would probably set up a small, isolated tent for her and the baby in the backyard.

Toward the middle of May there was a hot spell and she was miserable. Mel began sleeping on the pull-out couch in the living room in front of the fan because it was cooler. Though Bubba had air-conditioning, she didn't want him to run up a huge bill because of her. And she knew her fretful sleeping kept him up.

So she was surprised when he joined her one night.

"Can't sleep?" he asked as he sat down on the mattress.

"No. She just moves and moves. I know I should be grateful she's moving at all, but—"

"I'll rub your legs."

She wanted to cry. Here it had been *her* idea to get pregnant, *her* idea to enlist Bubba, *her* stupid brother who had kicked her out of the house next door and *her* laziness that had prevented her from finding an apartment instead of moving in with Bubba.

"It won't be much longer, Mel."

"I hope so. Bubba, don't you ever get fed up with this?"

He finished massaging one leg and started with the other. "The only thing that frustrates me is what you have to go through. It makes me feel so helpless, sometimes, because I don't know what to do for you."

Tears of shame stung her eyes. He was always thinking of her, and she was a constant crab—a bitch, really. He deserved someone calm and bovine, with a long, flowing white caftan and a wreath of flowers in her hair: one of those women in the soap operas who made it all look so easy. For one insane moment she considered renting one of their actresses for the last week, having Bubba tell everyone it was she, and hiding in the garage until everything was over.

"I miss just sleeping with you," she said softly.

"So do I. That's why I came downstairs." He finished massaging her leg and crawled into bed with her, his front to her back, his arms around her stomach— barely.

"You'll be up all night."

"Tomorrow's Saturday, we can sleep in together."

"Do you ever miss making love?" What a stupid question. *Of course* he missed it. She had lived with him long enough to know Bubba considered lovemaking one of the better pleasures life offered.

"I think about it. But we'll get that back, too."

"What was it like. Do you remember?" If she didn't joke she'd start to cry again.

"I remember everything about you."

"How about that stupid book the doctor recommended. Were there any helpful hints?"

She could hear the smile in his voice. "Go to sleep, Mel."

"You could just take my hand and kind of put it where you want it. It's one of the few parts of me that aren't fat."

"Oh, Mel." He hugged her against him and she felt the baby move. "There's so much more to it than that."

"Well, maybe if you thought of something else—"

"That's not what I'm talking about and you know it."

She wanted to turn around and fall asleep with her head on his shoulders like in the old days, but the thought of moving exhausted her.

"Do you ever regret this?" she whispered suddenly. It was the one question she'd wanted to ask him for so long, but she'd never had the courage.

"This?" He stroked her stomach gently. "No. Just think, Mel, if this hadn't happened, we'd still be best friends."

"And what are we now?" She needed reassurance and asked for it shamelessly.

"You're a part of my heart," he said simply.

She felt the single, solitary tear start to roll down her cheek. She didn't deserve this man. Beauty and the beast. His words had a softening effect on her; she felt her entire body relax. Even the baby quieted.

Mel took his hands in hers and pressed them against her stomach.

"How come you always know exactly the right thing to say?"

She could feel his smile against her shoulder. "That didn't come from the book, either."

THE BABY DROPPED, so Mel knew labor would be imminent. She spent the last days quietly, thinking more than anything else. She was fearful but prepared. Though she knew from talking to Sandy that no one practiced breathing exercises every night, with Bubba as her coach, she did. He timed her breathing, encouraged her, stayed very close. Neither of them left the house. He took his vacation to coincide with this time.

Bubba planned little things that wouldn't tax her strength, and one evening he invited Terry and Laurie over for a barbecue. A beginning-of-the-summer celebration, he called it. Though it was still only the middle of May and summer technically didn't begin until June 21, Mel liked the idea. Terry and Laurie were two people who hadn't pried and seemed genuinely glad to see her and Bubba together.

They had fixed barbecued chicken and potato salad; Mel had baked brownies, and Bubba threw together a vegetable dish and a fruit salad. But now she didn't feel like eating; she just wanted to lie in the hammock. The heat wave was over, and Mel was thankful as the cotton hammock swayed back and forth. A cool breeze washed over her as the sun slowly set.

Where her sudden burst of energy during the last few days had come from she couldn't imagine. Now all she really wanted was to get labor over with. Her back had been hurting since early that afternoon, and all she wanted to do was to get herself comfortably settled in the hammock, take the pressure off her legs and lower back. She thought of the end in sight as a relief. Nothing could possibly be as bad as waddling around with the belly she had.

Later she was standing next to Bubba, with his arm around her, when her water suddenly broke. She had the queerest sensation just a split second before it happened. Almost as if she knew.

It poured out onto the patio, soaking the cotton skirt of her loose dress, wrapping the light material around her legs. She knew without a doubt she was going into labor.

No. Wait a minute. Stop. I changed my mind.

But there was no turning back now. She began to walk—waddle—around the patio. The doctor had told her not to come to the hospital until the contractions were close together, until she couldn't walk or talk while having one. Mel knew from the books she'd read that it would be a while in coming. Bubba went inside and called the doctor to double-check and alert her that labor had begun. She knew he was going to run up to their bedroom and take the suitcase she'd packed two weeks ago and put it by the front door.

Terry and Laurie were excited for them and left shortly. It seemed they didn't want to intrude on such a private moment.

This isn't so bad, Mel thought as she felt another small contraction ripple through her. *I can handle this.* The early contractions had been so slight she hadn't realized she was going into labor. She smiled. For once in her pregnancy, something was turning out right.

Though Bubba protested, she did the dishes and put everything away. He set the patio to rights and covered the grill, then came back into the house and helped her finish up the cleaning.

"Don't wear yourself out. You'll need your strength for later."

She flashed a smile at him. "But I feel wonderful." *At last. Something you can do right.*

It was almost over. Was it a year ago she'd come to his door and asked for his help? It seemed longer. But now, probably within the next day, she'd see her baby. Know whether it was a boy or a girl. Hold it in her arms. Feel she'd accomplished something, know that all the discomfort and pain had a result.

Labor was going to be all right—she could feel it.

BY THE TIME they reached the hospital at almost one in the morning, the only thing Mel was sure of was that she was going to die.

When her doctor had said "Wait until you can't talk or stand," she hadn't been kidding. It was horrible. She knew from her reading and the Lamaze class that a normal contraction didn't last longer than thirty or forty-five seconds, but it seemed an eternity when she was in such pain. On the way to the car a powerful contraction had hit her, and she'd held onto Bubba's arm, practically crushing it, and panted like a dog—a very large Irish wolfhound.

They went straight to the emergency room and bypassed signing in. Thank God Bubba had had the foresight to drive her down two weeks before so she could fill out most of the lengthy forms. She knew she couldn't have done it in the condition she was in.

And if this is what it's like now, what will happen in transition? Transition sounded the same as a horrible roller coaster ride she'd been on the summer she was twelve. Donnie had dared her to go, so she'd stuck out her jaw stubbornly and bought a ticket. It had been too fast, racing up and down and around curves before she was ready for them. She held onto the rail until her knuckles were white, and she practically had to have her hands pried off. Then she staggered down from the loading platform and threw up. Donnie, bless his heart, laughed. Why did older brothers think stuff like that was funny?

What she'd learned in Lamaze was filtering in and out of her head, but she couldn't seem to get a handle on it. Thank God for Bubba. He stroked her forehead, talked to her, let her grip his hand during contractions, encouraged her to breathe throughout the haze of pain. His eyes were the only focal point she had.

When active labor began, she was glad they'd opted for a birthing room. She couldn't imagine her body being wheeled around, transferred from labor room to delivery room. She would have wanted to kill anyone who touched her. She felt as if her body didn't belong to her anymore, as if some alien spirit had invaded her and was pushing, pushing, making the contractions come stronger and stronger.

But they were strange, not one hard one after the other: first a hard one, then a soft one. Hard, then soft.

"Ask the nurse," she pleaded with Bubba after one of the hard ones. *Something's wrong. I know it.* As usual, nothing was going by the book. Who wrote those damn books, anyway? Probably the same cruel people who produced the commercials with the smiling madonnas.

Their nurse was a tall woman with brown hair. Desperately needing reassurance, Mel strained to hear what she had to say to Bubba. She felt so vulnerable, as if she were completely open, too weak to offer any resistance.

"I don't know. I've never seen anything like this."

Mel arched her head back and started to sob. *Never seen anything like this! Why, oh, why couldn't something in her pregnancy have been normal?*

BUBBA WAS WORRIED, but he had to stay calm. For Mel. He knew if he presented anything but confidence, it would be all over.

Damn the nurse for saying that in front of her! He knew she'd heard, knew by the way she started to cry as the woman left the room. It seemed cruel, what she was going through, the reality so different from what she'd been led to expect. He knew she wanted to have this baby naturally, and he wanted to go the distance with her, help her in any way he could.

Transition was what he dreaded most. What could be worse than what she'd already been through? He'd run marathons, swum long distances, exerted himself in any sport imaginable, yet he'd never seen anything like this. The physical endurance needed was incredible. As he wiped Mel's face and whispered words of encouragement, he wished desperately that he could share part of it with her, somehow ease her pain.

She was no coward. He knew she was scared, had known the entire last month she was convinced something was wrong because she was so big. He'd caught her crying a few times, but she'd never told him why. Now these strange contractions weren't helping.

But transition. Their Lamaze instructor had told them that it was the bridge between soft labor and active labor. The reason it was so painful was that dilation was rapid at that point, preparing for the crowning of the baby's head. The pain was so intense that sometimes a woman went a little out of her head.

"Don't be afraid if she does anything strange at this point," their instructor had said, talking softly to the couples all around her. "Transition is a major stress to the body, and women cope with it in different ways. I knew one woman who pummeled her husband with her fists and screamed at him."

And they'd all laughed nervously, convinced that nothing strange like that would happen to them.

But at this point, the way things are going, I'm not sure of anything anymore. He was brought out of his thoughts by the pressure of Mel's fingers against his. Another contraction was beginning. He put his face close to hers and began to breathe with her.

MEL WAS IN A HAZE OF PAIN. Nothing mattered anymore. Just as she'd failed every private test of pregnancy, so she was failing labor. She hated every television movie that had shown pregnant women, out on the ranch, twisting the bedclothes and heroically giving birth to a darling, squalling infant. She remembered the evening she and Bubba had watched a "Dynasty" rerun and saw Krystal Carrington give birth to Kristina. It all looked so simple on the screen. If they'd done it realistically, it would have had to be put on "The Twilight Zone."

The nurse bustled in. "Call for you, Mr. Williams. Anne Randell."

"I can't leave now," Bubba said softly.

"I'll stay with her," the nurse offered.

Mel managed a weak smile. "Go talk to my mom, Bubba. She's probably worried." Her mother had called her at home often during the past month; she had always had hunches, "feelings," about her daughters. When she couldn't reach her daughter by phone, she'd probably assumed they were at the hospital.

Mel watched him go, feeling some of her strength leave with him. She tried not to look at the nurse; she didn't want to give her any more chances to make remarks about what was normal and not normal.

She was lying on the bed, her shoulders propped up with pillows; her eyes closed when she heard the sound of rubber-soled feet on linoleum.

"Mrs. Murphy is in transition; she wants you to come see her for a second," the new arrival said to the brown-haired nurse.

Mel was almost glad to be left alone. None of this made sense. Were children really worth this? She felt tired and her thoughts were disjointed, but suddenly something flashed to the forefront of her mind.

I don't want to have this baby.

Another contraction hit her and she panted, her breathing completely erratic, and just let the pain take her.

Maybe I could ask Bubba to knock me out.

She stared at the far wall. There was a watercolor of an ocean scene, and she concentrated on the swirls of blue color. Another thought intruded, stronger than the first.

If I get out of the hospital now, I won't have to have this baby.

Why hadn't she thought of this before? Why hadn't Bubba? Of course! It all made perfect sense.

She sat up, reaching behind her to hold the hospital gown closed over her bare bottom, and contemplated the floor.

It's too far down. But Bubba had been sitting on a chair. If she could pull it over...

It was still too far down. Her unbalanced body made her clumsy. Mel glanced around, her energy born of a sudden desperation. Anything to escape the pain.

The bed table. Get the bed table. The stainless-steel bed tray. She looped her foot around it and pulled it over to the bed. Clumsily, she crawled on top of it. Then she felt around with her foot until her sole touched the chair.

This is going to work. She slowly climbed down into the chair and then shakily stood on the floor.

Now to the door. And freedom.

But as she started to walk, a contraction harder than any of the others hit her and she stopped, her legs trembling violently.

Leave the hospital—who are you kidding? Her plan, which had seemed so brilliant and logical seconds before, was torn to shambles. When the contraction lessened, she walked slowly back over to the chair and climbed into it. She rested for a second, then, panting from the exertion, heaved herself up on the bed tray. She'd be back in her bed before anyone was the wiser.

"Mel!" She looked over her shoulder and almost fell when she saw Bubba, a look of stark terror on his face, come rushing into the room.

He helped her get back into bed, fluffed the pillows underneath her shoulders and smoothed her hair out of her face.

"What were you trying to do?" He wasn't yelling, just asking.

"I thought if I got out of the hos—" Another contraction hit her and she reached for his hand. It peaked, and she crushed his fingers. This one was stronger than any of the others, and her fear must have showed on her face.

"Hold on to me, Mel. Breathe with me. Come on, breathe in."

Something inside her shattered, and to take its place came the complete conviction that she was never going to be able to have this baby, that she wouldn't make it through the rest of her labor.

"I can't make it, Bubba," she panted. "I can't do this." Her body was shaking violently, as if it had a life of its own. "I can't, I can't—"

"Mel, breathe—"

"Screw the breathing!"

"Mel, look at my face! I want you to breathe!"

"I can't!"

"Mel!"

"I can't, I can't!"

He pressed his face against hers, blew a breath out on her cheeks. "Come on, baby, you're almost there! Come on, Mel, don't give up now! Just a little longer—*breathe*!"

He became an extension of her, his breathing, his eyes, his love. There were people in the room now, and she opened her eyes and saw her doctor. The pressure was incredible, but she looked back at Bubba and kept breathing with him.

"You can push now, Melanie," her doctor said. "I want you to push right now."

She felt as if a ring of fire opened up on her body; all sensation focused where she knew the baby had to be.

"I see the head," the doctor said calmly. "That's good, Melanie; you're doing great. Push again."

And through it all she held onto Bubba's arm, his other hand supporting her shoulders as she curled slightly up.

Then she felt as if everything were sliding, sliding out. Her legs started to shake again with the effort.

"You have a little girl."

A girl! She started to cry and, looking up, was surprised to see tears running down Bubba's face. Even the doctor was crying.

"Is she all right? I want to hold her, I—" Another contraction silenced her. Something wasn't right. She still felt so full.

"Is that the afterbirth? There's something inside—" Looking at her doctor for confirmation, she was shocked to see surprise on the woman's face. Clutching Bubba, she closed her eyes.

Something's wrong. Oh, no. Oh, no!

She felt Bubba leave her and she opened her eyes. He'd walked down to the end of the bed and was talking with the doctor. His eyes were intense, anxious. Then she felt the same fire again. She clutched her fingers into fists, reaching for Bubba's hand, certain what happened after giving birth would surely kill her. There was more of that peculiar sliding sensation, then a baby's cry.

She couldn't open her eyes, afraid of what she might see. But she couldn't keep them closed. She looked up into Bubba's face, knowing he would tell her the truth.

"It's twins, Mel." He was holding a tiny baby and had the silliest, most idiotic grin stretched across his face. She felt herself begin to smile back.

"Two. Two babies?" She couldn't believe it, even though she saw them, a nurse holding one, Bubba the other.

"One was up behind the other. That's why we only heard one heartbeat," the doctor said.

She closed her eyes as she felt another nurse's hands press down on her abdomen. It hurt, and her eyes flew open again.

"Just a little more," the nurse said. "We're helping your uterus contract."

It seemed so unfair, after the rest of the pain. She forgot the babies, even Bubba, for a second as the nurse pushed again.

Bubba came around the side of the bed, holding one of the babies. "Two girls, Mel."

"Skip and Moondoggie," she said softly.

"Danielle and Alexandra," he replied.

She reached out for his hand as her eyes fluttered shut. She wanted to hold her children, count their fingers and toes, but she just didn't have the strength.

"Ten toes?" she mumbled.

"Twenty—ten on each."

"And their fingers?" She was drifting away from him and she squeezed his hand tighter.

"Perfect, Mel. They're absolutely perfect."

"I'm so glad."

And then, totally exhausted, she slept.

Chapter Thirteen

Bubba stumbled out into the waiting room, his body feeling strangely disconnected from his head. He'd followed the two nurses to the nursery and watched as they'd weighed and measured his daughters: four pounds, ten ounces; four pounds, eleven ounces. He couldn't remember how many inches long they were; he was that delirious with happiness.

And Mel was safe. He didn't blame her for falling asleep. He would have done the same thing. She'd had two! So even if she couldn't have any more children, they'd done the best they could.

He rubbed his hand wearily over the back of his neck. When he'd talked to Mel's mother, she had asked him quietly if he was the father. He'd admitted to it but had asked her not to tell Mel she knew. He'd assured her they were going to get married as soon as Mel decided she wanted to.

It was the beginning of a whole new life for them.

He glanced up as someone opened the door, and he smiled. Mr. and Mrs. Randell rushed into the waiting room, anxious looks on their faces. He took Mel's mother's hand and said, "Twins. Two little girls. And Mel is doing fine."

Tears misted Anne Randell's eyes. "Bless you for being with her, Bubba. It's the only reason Donnie didn't have an accident on the freeway coming up."

"Donnie?" His voice was slightly strangled. This didn't sound good.

"He's parking the car." She shook her head. "I didn't tell him. But you know, he's been moping around, and I think he's sorry for what he said to Mel. I couldn't bear to tell him he couldn't come, but I won't have him upsetting Melanie now." She looked like a fierce mother hen, and Bubba smiled. He felt so tired.

Donnie burst into the waiting room, and Bubba looked up again. His old friend *did* look slightly remorseful. Restrained. Maybe this would all work out for the best.

"Twins!" he shouted. The four of them were alone in the waiting room. Donnie looked incredulous for a moment.

"What were they?" he asked.

"Both girls."

"Did Melanie decide on any names?" her father asked.

He was tempted to tell them about Skip and Moon-doggie, but he didn't have the energy to laugh. What he wanted, more than anything, was to curl up next to Mel and go to sleep. But they hadn't thought of rooming in, so he'd have to settle for the next best thing and go home.

A nurse walked into the room, and Mel's mother rushed over to her.

"Can you tell me how my daughter's doing? Is she awake? Can we see her?"

The nurse smiled. "She's asleep. Twins are hard work. But I'll come out here and let you know the minute she wakes up." She turned to Bubba. "This guy worked really hard," she said, smiling.

"And we can't thank you enough, Bubba," Mel's father said.

"She wouldn't have made it without you," Donnie said with conviction.

Bubba didn't want to stand around and talk. He wanted to go home.

"You're exhausted," Mrs. Randell said. "Bubba, let Donald drive you home. We can pick up your car later."

The nurse touched his sleeve. "I just wanted you to know your babies are doing just fine. They're very healthy little girls, and you should be proud of yourself."

He could feel the dull flush creeping up his neck, but he nodded his head and looked back at Mel's family.

"You!" Donnie said, advancing on him slowly. "You son of a bitch, it was *you*!"

"Donald, stop!" Mrs. Randell said, a worried frown puckering her brow. "Bubba's worn out. He has to get home and sleep. You can discuss this later."

It was as if Donnie didn't even hear her. "I put her in that house next to you so you could *protect* her, not knock her up!"

"Donald!" This from Mr. Randell.

"I *trusted* you, you bastard!"

"Donnie, listen—" He didn't even see the fist that connected with his jaw. He just slumped to the floor.

You're a failure.

Mel slept through the twins' first feeding. The nurse told her she didn't have the heart to wake her up, so when she finally brought in the twins at six that evening, Mel was sitting up in bed, waiting for her daughters eagerly.

Her breasts hurt. She was so sore she had to sit on a cushion. But more than anything, she wanted to see the twins, hold them close.

Danielle—she thought it was Danielle—practically spit her nipple out. The nurse tried again, showing Mel how to stroke the tiny cheek with her nipple, but the baby fussed and started to cry.

"Maybe her sister," the nurse suggested. She unwrapped the second tiny bundle, flicked her feet gently to wake her, then handed her to Mel.

It was more of the same.

They hate me. They hate me because I didn't bond with them the minute they were born. They *did* seem more comfortable with the nurse. She bit her lip and handed her daughter back.

"I guess I'm not very good at this."

"Oh, no. We fed them in the nursery. They probably aren't even hungry."

They probably don't like me. "Can I hold them?"

"Of course."

Both babies simply slept, oblivious to who was touching them. Mel didn't dare wake them, suddenly realizing she had absolutely no idea what she was doing with two children.

The thought of taking care of them overwhelmed her. She'd have to start looking for another place to live. Bubba wouldn't—

But he would. She remembered the way he'd cried in the delivery room, the expression on his face when he'd looked down into his daughters' eyes.

"I'm still kind of tired," she admitted to the nurse.

"Of course you are," she said, taking the sleeping babies smoothly out of her arms. "I'll wake you for the next feeding."

"I'd appreciate that."

WHEN SHE WOKE UP AGAIN, Bubba was sitting in the chair next to her bed. One side of his face was discolored, a purple, shiny bruise prominent on his cheekbone.

"What happened?" She tried to scramble over toward him but winced as her body protested.

"Your brother and I had a little talk!"

"Donnie? Here? Oh, no!"

Bubba sighed. "He came up with your folks and overheard the nurse congratulating me. He figured out the rest for himself."

She touched his face gently, careful not to hurt him. Damn Donnie and his self-righteous attitude! Why couldn't he just leave them alone?

Bubba closed his eyes tiredly. "He thinks we should get married."

She stared at him, incredulous. The feelings of failure that had been washing over her since the birth of the twins finally culminated. *We should get married,* not *I want to marry you.* Well, no one else was going to run her life. Not now. Not ever.

"No." Her voice was low.

He opened his eyes. For a moment her heart went out to him, he looked so tired.

"Mel, it's different now. We have two other people to consider.

The babies. Donnie. The world. Damn it, Bubba, want me for myself. But why should he? She was the only woman she knew who got not one, but *two* chances to breastfeed—and blew both of them.

Why would he want an incompetent like her to mother his children?

"You can have them. I quit." There was nothing but quiet resignation in her voice.

"Mel, be reason—"

"Or we can give one to your mother and one to mine, and I'll move out and things will be just like when this all started."

"Things are never going to be that way again, Mel."

"Yes, they will. We'll make them that way."

He stood up shakily. "I'm going to go home now before we both say anything more we'll regret."

"You do that."

As soon as she heard his footsteps fade into the distance, she burst into tears.

WHAT HAD HAPPENED?

Bubba lay on the couch in his living room. He couldn't sleep. All he kept thinking about was the past twenty-four hours. He and Mel had been so close, had shared something so profound. Now they were further apart than when they'd started.

Why did Donnie have to come back into it? He had to settle things with his friend once and for all. What happened with him and Mel was none of her brother's conern. He had to make Donnie understand that.

What puzzled him was his friend's—his ex-friend's—attitude. He'd gone to college with Don, for God's sake! He knew what excesses his college buddy had been capable of.

The sharp knock brought him out of his moody thoughts, and he swung his legs over the side of the couch and walked slowly toward the door. If it was Don, he wasn't going to answer.

It was Joanie. He let her in, relieved that it was someone who was relatively uncomplicated. Joanie had accepted his love for Mel with a good-natured grace. She was currently dating a stockbroker, but he knew the guy bored her. Joanie liked a challenge.

"Where's Mel?" she asked, looking around.

"She's in the hospital."

Her eyes lit up. "Boy or girl?"

"Girls. Twins."

"That's great, Bubba! Congratulations!" She frowned. "You don't look too happy about it."

"I'm just tired."

"Don't pull that bull on me. Come on, spill it out."

So he told her, poured out everything he'd been thinking in the past hour. How he felt shut away from what was going on at the hospital. How Donnie was making himself a complete pain in the rear. How Mel had reacted when he'd asked her to marry him.

"I don't understand her. I just don't understand what she's thinking."

Joanie poured him a glass of wine. "Have you ever heard of the baby blues?"

For the next fifteen minutes, she filled him in on what she'd felt after her son was born. Joanie, married when she was seventeen and divorced shortly thereafter, told him all her feelings, her confusion.

"She probably thinks you asked her because of Donnie."

"That's ridiculous! She knows me better than that!"

"Bubba, women are never rational at a time like this. Wait, let me amend that. Maybe some women are, but not Mel. Not from what you've told me. Hell, sometimes one baby is frightening enough. Twins? She must be ready to slit her wrists."

When he looked up at her he was sure his terror showed in his expression.

"It was a figure of speech, Bubba. Mel isn't going anywhere. But I want to hear more about this Don character. Where does he get off telling the two of you how to run your lives? And why is he so hard on Mel?"

They talked for two hours, ordered out a pizza, talked some more. Then Joanie made him get in the hot tub with her and relax. Afterward, she dragged him back to the sofa and plopped him on it, bathing suit and all.

"Take your suit off as I go out the door, but wait until you hear the door shut. I don't want the Reverend Donnie to catch us together."

He smiled. He and Joanie had made the transition from light dating to friendship with ease. "You're a pal, Joanie."

"Sleep on it and call her in the morning, okay?"

MEL COULDN'T SLEEP.

She'd managed to do an adequate job of nursing the twins that night, and for a moment she'd wanted to call Bubba and share her feelings with him. But she remembered the look on his face as he'd slowly walked out of her room.

She'd cried for almost an hour after he left. One of the nurses had sat with her, held her hand, urged her to talk about her feelings. Then she'd told her it was quite normal to feel completely overwhelmed after the birth of a child—let alone two.

So now do you call him and apologize or hide in bed like a coward? Her hand was inching toward the phone when it rang.

Bubba? Her heart soared.

"Melanie. It's Donnie."

She felt sick to her stomach.

After listening to his harangue for two minutes, she said calmly, "Stuff it, Donald."

"What!" He was sputtering now, and she smiled. She'd been completely surprised when he'd backed off slightly the day of their argument. When had she realized her brother was ninety percent hot air?

"I said you can..." She described what he could do with himself in excruciating detail, then slammed the phone down into its cradle.

She felt wonderful. All those years of childhood tyranny: Donnie making her do things he knew scared her. "Come on, Mel, if you jump off the garage roof you'll fly."

Well, she was flying now. What an insecure little creep he'd been.

And he had nothing to do with Bubba's proposal. She felt more clearheaded after her cry, ready to pick up the pieces of her life and begin again.

Why not? She had a man who loved her, two beautiful daughters, a booming career, a supportive family—minus one—and enough energy to put things right again.

But most of all, she loved Bubba.

WHEN THE PHONE RANG he was so startled he fell off the couch.

"Hello. Who is this?" he asked belligerently, his words slurring slightly. Why was it he couldn't seem to get any sleep?

"Bubba?"

Mel. He fought his way out of the tangle of pillows and blankets Joanie had spread out on the couch and sat up. "Mel? Are you all right?"

"I'm fine, Bubba. A little ashamed of myself, but fine."

Was he hearing things? Was he talking again to the Mel he once knew? He clutched the receiver more tightly.

"About today..." she began.

"I phrased it all wrong, Mel. I didn't mean—"

"I know."

She knows. He closed his eyes and rested his forehead against his palm. The rest was going to be smooth sailing.

"So we still have that date we talked about?" he asked softly.

"As soon as I'm back to a size ten." Her voice lowered to a whisper. "I love you so much, Bubba. I just want to be beautiful for you again. I want you to be proud of me.''

"Aw, Mel." *Didn't she know?* "I already am.''

"THE BANNER GOES OVER the fireplace, and the balloons..." Bubba reached for the package of pink balloons and handed them to Joanie. "The balloons go everywhere. I want this place crazy with balloons.''

"I've got film in the camera; the cake's in the fridge; the nursery's ready; the quiche is in the oven—''

"Where's Henry?" Bubba asked suspiciously. His furry friend was usually never far away from food.

"He's sleeping in one of the cribs. He thinks you bought them both for him.''

"Wait till he sees the company he's getting. He'll wish we got that kitten instead." He gave Joanie a quick kiss. "Thanks. I'm going to leave now. Mel should be just about ready to check out.''

"Drive carefully, Daddy. Don't wrap your car around a tree.''

He blew her a kiss and rushed out the door.

What a guy, Joanie thought as she began to blow up a balloon. It touched her, the way Bubba was so involved. He was nothing at all like Mike had been—he hadn't even picked her up from the hospital. She'd been a frightened eighteen-year-old, knowing the only reason he'd married her was because she was pregnant.

Those days are behind you, she thought as she tied off the balloon and set it down on the couch. Within fifteen minutes she had several balloons blown up and the banner taped in place along one wall.

"Welcome home, Melanie, Skip and Moondoggie." She'd tried to make Bubba explain why he hadn't used the twins' real names—Danielle and Alexandra—but he'd simply laughed and pulled her hair, telling her he'd let her in on the joke when he brought Mel back.

He'd bought a special cake shaped like a surfboard. It was a little strange to her, considering the twins were still infants, but it made Bubba happy and that was what mattered.

When she heard the impatient knock on the door, she cursed and carried the balloon she'd been blowing up with her as she walked down the short hallway. Swinging the door open, she looked up into dark blue eyes.

"Hi." He was cute, a little reserved-looking, but his mouth hinted at a sensual nature. She'd met so many guys like this one she could peg him with a glance. Banked fires. Interesting.

"Is Bubba home?"

"No."

"Who are you?"

"I'm his maid," she replied sweetly, deliberately making it sound like a lie. Something about this man made her want to goad him.

"His maid? I don't...is Mel here?"

"She's coming home from the hospital today."

"Today? Why wasn't she home sooner?"

He was a nosy one. Here he was, expecting her to give him everyone's life story on the front steps, and she still had a million balloons to blow up and a quiche in the oven.

"They give you a little more time with twins." She smiled slowly. "Why don't you come in..."

"Donnie."

Donnie. This was *really* interesting—much more so than Mark the stockbroker. "Why don't you come on in and wait for them, Donnie? I'm sure they'll be glad to see you." As she remembered Bubba's anguished night after Donnie had interfered, an amusing little plan began to form in her mind. *Oh, Joanie, you'll fry in hell for this one.*

He followed her inside, and she started him blowing up balloons.

"Would you like a drink, Don?"

"Rum and Coke, if you've got it."

She filled the glass to the brim with rum and added a splash of Coke for color. As she handed it to him, she said cheerfully, "Just let me check what's in the oven and I'll be right back. This'll be a fun party, huh?" She was aware of his eyeing her body. She didn't mind. She'd met Bubba at the health club, and they'd gotten along because of their interest in physical fitness. Joanie was proud of what she'd made of her life, and one of the things that made her proudest was that she looked damn good.

She went into the kitchen, tested the quiche, pulled it out and set it on top of the oven. *So far, so good.* Walking back out into the living room, she took a quick glance at Don's glass. Half empty. Great.

Slowly, with great deliberation, she peeled her cotton sweater over her head. "It's hot in here, don't you think, Don? Should I turn on the air conditioner or what?" She knew the bikini top she had on underneath barely concealed her full breasts. She watched the way his eyes slowly devoured her. *Men can be so predictable at times.*

She arched her back slightly, enough to make her breasts strain against the cotton suit top. "Maybe not." Swaying her hips just a little more than was normal, she waltzed over to the couch and sat down close to him. She picked up a balloon. "I just can't seem to blow hard enough. Will you do these for me?"

He was hooked. His eyes had that slightly glazed look. With any luck, Mel and Bubba would walk in that door within thirty minutes. She had plenty of time.

She touched the corner of his mouth with the tip of her finger and smiled. "You have the most sensuous mouth, you know that?"

MEL GOT OUT OF THE CAR, walking slowly, carefully, Alexandra in her arms. Bubba had Danielle. Together, the four of them came up the driveway toward the front door of Bubba's house.

"Just what do you have planned, Bubba?" she asked. He'd looked as if he were about to pop the entire time they drove home. Now his hand was fumbling with the key, and she knew he had something in store for her.

"Something I hope you remember forever." He kissed her forehead, then swung open the door.

As they entered the living room, the first thing Mel saw was the banner. Then the balloons. She squeezed Bubba's arms and was about to say something when she heard a slight, scuffling noise.

Then a voice. Low. Intense.

"Oh, yeah. Like that—just like that. Oh, Joanie—"

"Joanie?" Bubba asked loudly.

To Mel's horror, she saw her brother's disheveled head bob up from behind the couch. As she watched, he began to scramble around for his pants. It took her befuddled mind a moment to register that Donnie didn't have any clothes on.

"Donald!" Bubba said loudly, setting Danielle down in one of the living-room chairs. "On my living-room rug—and with one of my best friends! How could you do this to me, to Mel!"

Donnie was buttoning his shirt, his eyes darting from Mel's face to Bubba's. Then Joanie sat up, the afghan pulled around her bare shoulders. When Donnie wasn't looking, Mel was amazed to see her flash a triumphant smile at Bubba.

She set the whole thing up. Mel started to laugh, great choking gasps that came out from her stomach. Donnie looked like a crazed chicken, dancing around the living room and grabbing his shoes and socks.

She decided to play her part. "And in front of the children! My God, Donald, you have no shame at all?"

He ran out the door, slamming it after him, and Mel walked quickly around the couch and collapsed, Alexandra still in her arms. But the baby was waking up, her clear blue eyes blinking.

"Oh, Mel, she's gorgeous," Joanie said softly. "Where's her little sister?"

"Right here." Bubba handed her the other twin and Mel smiled. Joanie looked so funny, wrapped in the afghan and holding a baby.

"What was Donnie doing here? I mean..." Suddenly Mel was embarrassed.

"Hey, he had it coming, after all he did to the two of you." Joanie frowned. "I hope you aren't mad, Mel." Now she sounded uncertain.

"Are you kidding? I used to fantasize about moments like this! I loved it!"

"I didn't get all the balloons blown up, Bubba."

"Hey, Joanie, I forgive you." Bubba ruffled the top of her head. "Now let's get going—we have a party to start!"

"I just want an answer to one question," Joanie said, gazing down at the sleepy infant in her arms. "Which one of these little guys did you name Moondoggie?"

THEY WERE MARRIED on the Fourth of July, fourteen months after the twins were born. Mel and her mother had made her wedding dress; Alicia and her sisters were the bridesmaids, Joanie her matron of honor. Terry was the best man. Jonathan was there as well, looking very proud. Mel even tied a blue ribbon around Henry's neck, and he fought furiously with it until the smells of cooking food distracted him. Bubba's garden was alive with flowers Mel had planted, and afterward, they had a huge barbecue and invited the entire neighborhood.

After the wedding, Sandy took the twins for the weekend. Henry was confined to the kitchen with a large piece of barbecued chicken, and when the last guest left, Bubba locked up the house and raced upstairs.

"Alone at last!" he said, sweeping her into his arms Rudolph Valentino-style.

She couldn't stop giggling. All the champagne she'd drunk had rushed straight to her head. "Do you want to go down to the beach and see the fireworks?" she asked.

"I think I'd rather create some fireworks of my own." He wiggled his eyebrows à la Groucho Marx. "Now are you going to take that gown off or am I going to have to rip it off your body?"

"I'll take it off. I'll take it off!"

She retreated to the bathroom and changed into something she'd saved especially for her husband: a black silk nightgown, shaped like a slip and cut on the bias. The garment molded her body like a second skin. She unwound her hair, brushed it out, then took one of the white gardenias she'd brought up from the garden and stuck it behind her ear.

Perfect. She hadn't wanted anything demure for tonight. It was much more fun anticipating Bubba's reaction to this.

He was lying underneath the covers when she walked back in, and his eyes lit up when he saw her.

"Wow."

All she'd wanted in the way of his reaction was in his face. Walking slowly toward him, she let the silk ripple sensuously against her body.

"Fireworks, huh?" she whispered, just before she cupped his face in her hands and lowered her mouth to his.

Fireworks. Just in his kiss. No one had ever kissed her like Bubba, and when he broke away she sighed her pleasure and twined her arms around his neck.

"I know this is an inopportune moment, but I have one more wedding present for you."

She looked at him, confused for a moment. What more could he possibly give her?

But he was up out of the bed; then he took a piece of paper from the dresser drawer. When he handed it to her, he was smiling broadly.

She couldn't believe what was in front of her: the deed to the house next door.

"I bought it from Donnie."

"Oh, Bubba." The little house she'd loved. The bedroom where they'd first made love. Her garden.

"I figured it was insurance against having him as a neighbor."

She started to laugh. "Oh, come on, Bubba. Joanie's mellowed him out, don't you think?"

"Yeah, but she didn't have to marry him!"

They both laughed, remembering Donnie dancing around downstairs, trying to find his clothing.

"Anyway, it's a tactical move, too. When the girls get old enough—say, twelve or thirteen—we can move next door. That way we can have our own phone and refrigerator."

"Uh-huh." She began to kiss his neck, her fingers tracing the muscles in his chest.

"And a little privacy."

"Hmm." She nuzzled the soft skin underneath his ear with her lips, then kissed his jaw.

"When they have their friends over, they can play their music as loud as they want."

She slid her body against his, delighting in the feel of his arousal.

"And their boyfriends can stay over—"

She stopped nuzzling and looked him straight in the eye.

He smiled that quick, confident grin she loved. "Just checking to see if you were listening."

"Very funny. No, Alex and Dani are going to do things the right way. None of the crazy stuff we did."

"Oh, Mel." Bubba rolled his eyes. "I was afraid of this. Marriage has made you boring."

"Boring?" She scrambled up in bed, peeling the silken gown over her head and throwing it on the side of the large bed. "Boring?" She took the flower out of her hair, trying not to laugh. "*I'll* show you *boring*!"

She covered his body with hers, loving the feel of his bare skin against hers. Looking down into her husband's eyes, she whispered a sensual command.

"Now kiss me, you wild and crazy fool."

Bubba was more than happy to oblige.

Harlequin American Romance

COMING NEXT MONTH

#137 CONVICTIONS by Beverly Sommers

Madelyn never expected to find Eddie on her doorstep. They had been pen pals for three years, but he had never told her, in his letters, that he was being released from prison. Nor, she realized, what crime he had committed. Now that he was out, what did he want from her?

#138 THE EDGE OF FOREVER by Barbara Bretton

Meg Lindstrom feared success. Years ago she put down her camera after her sister's heroic death. Now at the bequest of her mentor, Meg has one last job to do. Only Meg never planned on working with novelist Joe Alessio—a man who will challenge both her talent and her heart.

#139 JACKPOT by Judith Arnold

Money. A river of it poured from the slot machine and pooled at Lucia's feet. Cameras clicked, a crowd gathered and Lucia felt ill. She didn't want the money; it brought out people's greed. Like the stranger beside her. Was he taking charge of her and her newfound wealth—or was he taking *advantage* of them?

#140 EVER SINCE EVE by Pamela Browning

Blacklisted by the mill owners, Eve had exhausted all conventional options. What Derek and Kelly Lang offered was not precisely a job but more a service they needed rendered. All Eve had to do was sign the papers that would bind her to the Langs for at least nine months—the time it would take to carry their child to term.

Take 4 novels and a surprise gift FREE